Thorns of the Rose

A contemporary love story

Ted Tillotson

Thorns of the Rose

Published by Dragon Lair Books

Avenal, California

http://www.tedtillotsondragonlairbooks.com

This is a work of fiction. Names, characters, places, and incidents either are the product of the author's imagination or are used fictionally. Any resemblance to actual persons, living or dead, events, or locals is entirely coincidental.

Book design by Lord Dragon

ISBN 978-0615470474

Printed in the United States of America

Also By Ted Tillotson

Available on Amazon.com and other retail outlets

Deathmaker – a dark psychological thriller

**Published by Omega Publications
Palm Springs, CA**

* * * *

The Magic Meadow
Kayla's fantasy

Published by
Dragon Lair Books

Avenal, California

* * * *

Thorns of the Rose

* * * *

This book is dedicated to my late wife,

Barbara

1949 to 2008

She was always supportive

* * * *

"If you have faith, anything is possible."

The author, March 2011

* * * *

* * * *

Many thanks to my editor,

Norma Howell

She was tough, and usually right.

* * * *

Thorns of the Rose

A rosebud sleeps quietly until its time, then
bursts open for all to admire.
The petals are velvet, rich with color and
scent.
So beautiful is the rose, so perfect in its form
and shape.
Beware this flower--it tops a stem bearing
thorns of fire.
Treat it carelessly; ignore the warning, and
the sting of thorns you'll not escape.
As the rose, so is life.
As with life and the rose, so is love.
Beware the thorns, know where they are,
don't touch them, and your dreams will not
be taken away.

Thorns of the Rose

Prologue

Four gray and white seagulls circled around the child. Each bird flew closer to the girl's outstretched hand. She giggled when a gull snatched the treat.

Mrs. Clara Nelson stayed back and watched. "Be careful they don't nip your fingers."

"They're my friends. I won't get bit." She held out another large potato chip and a pair of small gulls squawked and went for it at the same time. "Don't fight. I'll get more."

"I don't think we have any left, honey."

"There's a bag in the cupboard on the patio."

"Let's wait until your mother gets home."

"I'll be okay. Would you get them for me, please?"

"You promise to stay where you are?"

"Promise—double."

Clara trudged up the slight incline toward the rear of the split-level house. She heard loud squawking and glanced back.

Two large seagulls started attacking the girl to get at the bag of chips.

"Don't fight—I'm getting more." The biggest bird bit her hand. She jerked her arm away. The child's elbow hit the switch. The wheelchair shot forward and to the right. It toppled off the wooden ramp and pinned her under it.

"Nancy!" Mrs. Nelson ran to the girl and stepped down off the ramp. "Oh, my God!" Clara could not lift the heavy chair.

Nancy did not move.

* * * *

Thorns of the Rose

Chapter One
Two Different Worlds
(Mid-spring 1978)

CHILDREN'S HOSPITAL
SAN DIEGO, CA – 5:30 PM:

Carolyn stared out of the third floor window at the snarled traffic on northbound 163. She had paced the small waiting room more than a dozen times during the past two hours. Her neighbor, Mrs. Clara Nelson, sat near the door cleaning her glasses. Her eyes were rimmed with tears. "I only left her for two minutes."

"It's not your fault." Carolyn turned away from the window and sat beside Clara. "Nancy's old enough to know better."

Mrs. Nelson blotted her eyes with a fresh tissue. "She loves those birds so ...." She shuddered and clutched Carolyn's hand. "I'll never forget the fright when I saw the poor child crumpled in the sand with her wheelchair on top of her. Dear God, I'm so sorry."

Carolyn blinked back tears of her own "Me too." Her voice shook. "The fault is mine, Clara." *All of it,* she thought. *Every day of Nancy's eleven crippled years are my doing. I brought her into this world, and I put her in that chair.* The memory came back whispering those nightmare words.

Ms. Parker, I'm afraid your daughter has spina bifida.

* * * *

Dr. Bailey and another physician stepped into the room. Dr. Bailey said, "Nancy's in recovery, she's going to be all right. The break isn't as bad as you might've thought."

Mrs. Nelson took a quick breath. "Thank God."

The doctor said, "I'd like you both to meet Dr. Harold Stone, our orthopedic surgeon. Dr Stone, Carolyn Parker, Nancy's mother. And this is Mrs. Clara Nelson, Nancy's *almost* grandmother and caregiver."

Clara flushed. "I didn't give enough care today, did I?"

Carolyn said, "That isn't the least bit true." She smiled and shook the doctor's hand.

He nodded. "I'm pleased to meet both of you."

Carolyn looked at Dr. Bailey. "Can we see her?"

"Let's hear from Dr. Stone first."

* * * *

UNIVERSITY OF CALIFORNIA, SAN DIEGO: 5:45 PM:

John Freeman lugged his gym bag across the nearly deserted outdoor student information center. At midday the multilevel complex would be a mass of people, a bedlam of sounds and smells. The center echoed the voices of future researchers, teachers, doctors and lawyers. This late in the day it would be quiet.

"Mr. Freeman?"

John turned back and looked down into the center. A tall lanky young man jogged toward him. *James Peterson. He'd failed tryouts for the track team this afternoon.* John felt uneasy. He smiled to hide it. "You caught me."

"Yeah, I saw you go by. I was in the coffee shop."

John set his bag down. "You want another shot, right?"

"Let me try again tomorrow. I can make it, I know I can. I was off today. Please, Mr. Freeman, one more chance."

"It's up to Coach Lawrence, Jim, not me."

"You're his assistant, you got his ear. I need the scholarship. If I can't get it in track, I don't get it."

John leaned against the wrought iron railing near the top of the last few steps. He looked up at the banner above the entrance of the two-story student bookstore. *Cal Markham for student body president!* It was the hope of another young man seeking a place, a position of meaning. John Freeman sought the same thing. He didn't know where or what it would be. "I'm a student teacher, not an assistant coach."

"I need another try, Mr. Freeman. Talk to Professor Lawrence, I'll be there. Let me run against one of the team guys." Jim struggled with his frustration. "I'm a chemistry major. If I can't get the scholarship, I won't make my degree." The young lad shook his head. "The track team is my only chance."

The plea poked at John like a sharp knife. *Why does it fall on me to grant Jim another chance when there's no one to plead my case?*

Christine's voice grated across the back of John's mind. *We're through, John. I can't deal with you anymore.*

"Okay, Peterson. Forget today, you were off, out of sorts. Be at the track at 2:00 PM sharp. I'll test you myself. You'd better run your young ass off."

"You bet I'll be there—I'll tear that track to dust!"

"The coach makes the final decision, not me."

"I know." He shook John's hand. "Thank you."

"I'll talk to Lawrence after morning workouts. I suggest you prepare for a tougher test."

"Mr. Freeman, I'll give you everything I've got."

"You'll have to." He watched the young man sprint away. John grabbed his bag and stared back into the empty student center and whispered, "I gave it all too."

Christine's rage echoed in his head again. It felt like fingernails scraping a blackboard. *I gave you my best, you sonofabitch! You didn't give me shit!*

* * * *

CHILDREN'S HOSPITAL – 6:00 PM:

Carolyn squeezed Mrs. Nelson's shoulder to comfort herself and the older woman.

Dr. Stone said, "Given Nancy's condition, healing will be understandably slower than usual." He glanced at Dr. Bailey. "Chuck tells me she's quite the fighter.

Carolyn nodded. "I'm concerned about the pin. The child's crippled enough."

Dr. Stone held up his hand. "Nancy will have full use of her arm. It will be as strong as ever, maybe stronger. She's right-handed, so driving her chair will be no problem while the break heals."

Still upset, Clara Nelson shuddered and cried again. "That poor child, she hurts so much ...."

Carolyn looked at Dr. Bailey. "Charles, you're sure about her hip and spine?"

He sat back and crossed his legs. "The bruises on her upper left thigh will appear worse than they are. And they'll take some time to fade away. The tumble did jar her lumbar region, but there's no detectable injury to the ménages membranes. You have my word on that."

She shook her head. "I'm sorry ... it just frightens me."

The doctor leaned forward and took her hand. "Nancy will always get the best I can give her."

"I know that, I'm ... I don't know what I am."

"A very concerned mother, I think." He grinned and squeezed her hand.

Clara wiped her eyes. "Can we see her?"

Dr Stone stood. "Sure, but just for a few minutes." He looked at Carolyn. "Ms. Parker, I'd like to admit Nancy for a couple of days."

"Is there a problem?"

"Not at all. I want to keep an eye on her arm and get to know her a little more."

Dr. Bailey said, "Let's look in on our prize patient."

* * * *

SOUTH LA JOLLA SHORES – SAN DIEGO – 6:25 PM:

John parked his beat-up yellow VW-bug in the carport, dragged the gym bag with him and climbed out. He dropped the bag on the back steps, grabbed his mail from the letter box and unlocked the door to his rented beach house.

The odor of leftover bacon hit him. "Dishes before dinner."

The blinking red light on the answering machine caught his eye. He slid the bag against the wall by the door, tossed the mail on the cluttered coffee table and pressed play.

Sonny, it's your mother. I hate these things.

"Now what?" He cleared a space and sat on the frayed couch and listened to his mother's message.

Call me. You know how I get when I don't hear.

John looked through his mail and let the phone messages run.

Hey, Gov, Tony Cambella here. Christ, it's been a hundred years. Call the office, I'll make time. Good to hear from you. We gotta do lunch. Ciao.

"Yeah, right. I called a week ago." He studied an envelope from *Harding, Fowler & Whyler.* Christine's attorneys. "Shit!" The next message was from Chris.

By now you should've received a letter from my lawyer. I'm fed up, John. I had to run your check twice. You're late again. I'm taking you to court. I've had it!

He ripped the letter open. "Dammit!" It was a summons.

Another message scratched through the small speaker:

Hi, Johnny, it's Timmy. I guess you're mad. If you're gonna run tomorrow, I'll be there, I promise. I'm sorry I couldn't make it yesterday.

John fought the urge to tear up the summons and stared at the phone. "I'm angry, big guy, but not with you."

* * * *

CHILDREN'S HOSPITAL – 6:40 PM:

Nancy Parker, groggy from the operation, had tearfully hugged Mrs. Nelson and now gripped her mother's hand. Her lower lip quivered. She looked for signs of anger in Carolyn's eyes. "I'm sorry, Mommy. I just wanted to feed my friends. I didn't mean to be bad."

Carolyn smiled, held back tears and waited for the pressure in her throat to slip away. "You weren't bad, sweetheart, I don't think that. Not for a second."

Dr. Bailey reached over and took Nancy's right wrist. He watched her expressions while reading her pulse. "By gosh, she's still alive."

With effort, Nancy grinned. "I only broke my arm, not my head."

The doctor said, "Thank goodness. What could we do for a broken head?"

Nancy turned toward the stranger in the room. She blinked, tried to wet her dry lips with her coated tongue. She glanced at the cast on her arm, then back to the doctor.

He smiled. "I'm Dr. Stone. I put that thing on you."

She blinked rapidly, studied the cast, shifted her eyes to Dr. Bailey, then to her mother. "I'm sorry, Momma ... I'm sorry." She couldn't hold back her tears.

"It's okay, honey." Carolyn brushed strands of strawberry blonde hair off Nancy's forehead. Without looking at Dr. Stone she said, "She's very aware of hospital and medical procedures, Dr. She knows you're a specialist and she's well aware of what that means."

Nancy looked up at Dr. Bailey. "Can't you take care of me?"

He patted her right hand. "I will always take care of you. Dr. Stone just happens to know more about broken bones than I do."

The child studied the surgeon. "You cost extra." Her voice quavered, "My mom can't really afford a special doctor."

Carolyn squeezed her daughter's

shoulder. "That's not our concern right now."

"It is, Mom. It always is! I did it this time. I'm the one who did it."

Clara Nelson sniffed and left the room.

Dr. Bailey met Carolyn's eyes and mouthed the word, *insurance.*

She adjusted Nancy's pillows. "Dr. Stone is covered by our insurance."

The child tried to sit up, but couldn't. "You're free?"

Dr Stone laughed. "I guess I come with the policy." He leaned forward and took Nancy's right hand. "Can we be friends?"

"I guess ... maybe."

"Great. I need to keep an eye on what's happening inside that cast."

"Can I see too?"

"We'll look at it together."

Nancy grinned, wet her lips again. She nodded. "We can be friends."

Carolyn swallowed the burning in her throat and caught Dr. Bailey's eyes. "Okay, little lady. How about a private room with your very own TV?"

Nancy's face lit up. "Really?"

Her mother blinked rapidly and nodded. *My Nancy can't walk because I rode the sixties to the Max.* She pushed a few strands of hair off the child's forehead. "Absolutely, sweetheart, but you have to make a promise."

"Anything for my own TV." Her eyelids started drooping.

"Promise to rest, mind the nurses and turn off the TV when they say. We got a deal?"

"Deal. I'll be the best patient in the whole place. I promise ...." The effects of the emotional visit and the drugs were taking their toll. "I feel sleepy."

Carolyn shivered. She remembered all too vividly the many times she had slipped away into a deep black void.

* * * *

LA JOLLA SHORES – 7:00 PM:

John Freeman clutched the summons and whispered, "How on earth could love rot into such resentment and hate?"

* * * *

Outside, loud waves crashed onto the shore. Each one took back something the sea had given just a moment before.

* * * *

Chapter Two
Men also cry

Cold, gray fog covered La Jolla Shores like a massive blanket of dense muslin. It fought and rolled as the sun began to chase it into the ocean.

Ghostly figures of walkers and joggers slipped north and south through the eerie dampness, each padding along toward individual goals. John Freeman was among them. *His* brass ring loomed ahead, just out of reach.

Running was his therapy, a way to focus, align priorities, shed the past and put the future in perspective. Vietnam was long dead, though it occasionally crawled from the grave seething, grinning, *hissing* its way into fitful, dark sleep.

* * * *

The 1976 divorce, now two years old, held hands with failure in John's mind. No day passed without thoughts of Christine. Those memories infected what few relationships he'd had since.

"To hell with her!" John shouted, through clenched teeth and controlled breaths. "Goddamned to hell with her!" He ran faster, pushed harder.

The curse was filled with anger, as it was every day he ran. Before noon John would swear at himself for cursing his ex-wife and take the blame for the failed marriage.

He continued south, running faster on the wet sand. Cold spray wet his legs. It felt good.

The brooding shape of his rented beach house appeared in the thinning fog. He pumped harder through the last twenty-five yards.

Grunting, out of breath, John grabbed the front porch railing. "Damn. I'll kill myself yet."

Long, misty rays of sun rode on blue-green waves to shore and spread with them over the sand.

In the distance a young couple walked hand-in-hand toward some tomorrow they'd promised each other in the touching and loving of the night before. John watched, catching his breath.

I'll always love you.

Christine's broken vow echoed in his head

Crashing waves pushed wide fans of sunlit foam higher onto the beach. The patterns reminded John of Christine's long hair falling over his face in the middle of a cool night. A time filled with closeness, warm breath and love.

A dog barked, splashed into the surf. The memory fell away, remaining on the floor of John's mind like shattered glass that hadn't been swept away.

"Hi, Johnny!" The young voice rose above the surf. Timmy Collins ran toward him from a swirl of fading mist.

John pulled the red sweatband off his head and ran his hand through his hair. "Is this a strange creature from the killer fog I see?" He changed his sullen expression into a bright, wide smile. "No, I guess it's a kid I once knew named Timmy."

The boy ran up to him puffing.

"Sorry, Johnny. I couldn't make it the last couple days." Timmy leaned forward resting his hands on his legs and caught his breath.

"Days?" John, pulled a ring of keys from the pocket of his trunks. "Young man," His tone became fatherly, "we haven't worked out together for more than a week. Looks like you tried to make up for it one shot."

The boy straightened. “Yeah,” he mumbled on a short breath. He looked at John and let go of his smile. "I been kinda helping my mom. She has to get my sister ready for day school an' all." He shifted his eyes away and rested both arms on the porch railing.

There was more to tell.

John reached over and ruffled the boy's hair. "That's great. I'm proud of you." He sat on the porch steps and wiped the sleeve of his shirt across his face. *Yeah, I can dig it, Timmy,* thought John. He stared out over the hazy beach. *Kid barely turns twelve and his father packs UP and splits—some birthday present.*

"Hey!" John turned toward the boy and saw him still burning a hole in the porch floor with his eyes, scuffing a Nike in the sand. "How's things with you and your dad?"

A long silence.

"Ain't seen him in a while ...." His voice shook. A single tear fell from the lad's face.

"Well, engineers get pretty busy at this time of the year, Tim."

The boy sniffed, spoke in broken words. "It ain't his damn job."

More tears.

"What's wrong Timmy?" John stood and put his arm around the boy's shoulders.

"He's got a girlfriend." Timmy's voice filled with anger and pain. "Bitch! She lives in L.A. Damn her!" The boy's hurt came straight from the center of his heart.

"Let it out, Tim." John put both arms around his young friend and held him. "It was bound to happen sooner or later. We talked about that, remember?"

"Yeah ...." Timmy sobbed, took a short breath. "The bitch doesn't want nothin' to do with kids."

John held the boy tighter, felt the child's ache rush through himself. "She could change her mind, Timmy. Women do that a lot."

The boy pulled away and looked into John's eyes. "No she won't! Not her." Snot ran over Timmy's upper lip, his eyes were full of hurt.

"Okay. It's a bad deal, but you still have your dad." John brushed locks of sweaty hair out of Timmy's burning eyes.

The boy's sobs heaved out words as if he'd been badly frightened by a cold voice from a midnight closet. "My dad called last night. He said we could plan on being together every two months." He swallowed hard. "Two lousy days every eight weeks." He gulped again and pressed his face into John's shirt. "Why'd she take my dad away, Johnny? Why?"

The surf sparkled with beautiful sun-powered stars and roared onto the beach.

It's life, Timmy, good old dads go away

and find other women. Dear moms slip out to the Seven-Eleven and never come back. Buck UP *kid, we're living in a time where commitment doesn't mean a hill-a-shit. Welcome to the club. To be a member, someone you love has to tell you to fuck-off.*

John locked the door on the thought and hugged the boy harder.

"I know it hurts, Tim. It'll cut more before it stops." Tears fell into the boy's hair from John's eyes. "You got me Tim--don't forget it."

Timmy's crying eased. "I know ... thanks." His voice was thick with bitter sorrow. He hung on to his man-friend like a small child who'd been lost in a dark forest and finally found. "I feel dumb ... cryin' all over you like a baby." The boy hugged John as hard as he could.

"Easy, Champ—you'11 crack my ribs." He laughed and blinked back further tears. He held Timmy away from him and smiled. "Here, let's clear all this away." John lifted the bottom of his sweatshirt and wiped the boy's face.

"I love you, Johnny." Timmy cut his words as though he had said the wrong thing.

"Yeah, I know, I love you too." John's eyes watered again.

"Hello." The female voice sounded close.

John looked up, Timmy turned to see who it was.

"Is Timmy all right?"

"Hi!" said the boy, smiling again.

"He's fine." John quickly wiped his face on the already saturated sweatshirt. "He's great, right?" He laughed, then ruffled Tim's sandy, brown hair.

"Yeah, I'm okay." Timmy wiped his eyes and made streaks across his face.

"I saw you two as I ran by. I thought--" The woman looked at John, then to Timmy. "Well, I thought maybe, something was wrong." She stopped and looked away, changing the subject. "Nice morning."

John cleared his throat. "Beautiful."

"Tim?" She looked at John again, "Aren't you going to introduce us?" She pushed several strands of shiny, curly auburn hair away from her face. Her deep, brown eyes sparkled.

"Sure." answered Timmy and brushed his face again with a nervous hand. "This is my friend. John Freeman. We run together a lot an' talk and stuff."

"I'm Carolyn Parker." She moved closer, held out her slender hand. Her nails were perfect and polished in deep salmon.

"Hi." John adjusted his sweatshirt around the top of his trunks. *She's beautiful. Familiar.* "You run here a lot?"

"Now and then." Her hair swept over her shoulders in the ocean breeze. Reddish highlights apparent in the early sun. She shook John's hand. "Timmy and I just met this morning while he was looking for you." Carolyn let go of John's hand. "Now you're found." She smiled. Her eyes didn't.

"I think we found each other." John realized he was staring. To the boy he said, "Didn't we, Champ?"

"I guess so." Timmy glanced at the sports watch he got from his dad the same day he learned about the *bitch* in L.A. "Gotta go. My mom's gonna kill me." The watch offered more information than the boy could use. It could calculate time-to-miles, or the other way around. Instead of reminding the boy of his father, the gift-watch brought up the memory of the *woman* in Los Angeles. He shook hands with Carolyn, because it seemed like the right thing. "Let's do it again, okay?"

She laughed. This time her eyes did too. "We will. Nice meeting you."

"Oh, yeah!" Tim's face lit up. He turned to John. "I'm pitching Sunday against the Tigers. Can you come, Johnny? It's a big game."

"I'd like to, but you know I'm going away for a while." John caught Carolyn's eyes and felt something. A feeling that starts deep inside, rises up and crashes against the hollows of the mind. *I have to know her.*

Timmy said, "I could pitch a winner if you were there." The boy's excited eyes looked straight into John's. "Please, Johnny." No trace of tears remained on his innocent face, but a deep ache throbbed inside. His father *wouldn't* see the game, but Johnny *could.*

"Having me there decides the game?"

Timmy grinned from ear-to-ear. "You bet your butt!"

John's eyes stung. He was important to the boy. There could be only one answer. "You got it, Champ."

Timmy jumped and screamed at the same time. "Great!"

John swallowed hard. He took the boy by the shoulders. "Count on it—that's an absolute promise."

"Even if you're gettin' ready to go?"

With a tremor in his voice, John said, "I'll be there."

Timmy threw his arms around his man-friend in a serious bear hug. "Far out!" For the moment, all thoughts of his father's bad news and the *lady* in L.A. were gone. He gave John a final squeeze. "I gotta go."

Carolyn checked her watch. "I'm late. Nice meeting you both." She pulled her hair back, slipped on a bright, yellow headband. "Which way you headed, Timmy?"

He pointed north. "That-a-way."

Carolyn laughed. "Okay, Captain Kirk. Let's go."

John felt a sudden, small panic. "Listen, I run here, usually with Timmy, most mornings. Maybe you could join us."

The boy responded first. "That'd be cool."

Carolyn grinned at Timmy. "I usually run farther north, but maybe. What time?"

"Around five-thirty. Even in the rain." He laughed. "Tomorrow for sure." Their eyes met briefly. *She's considering it,* he thought. "The three of us. We can race."

The boy said, "Yeah, we'll have a blast!"

Ocean wind gusted off the surf pushing Carolyn's hair away from her neck. Her loose-fitting, yellow and blue, *Chargers* sweatshirt pressed against her firm figure. "I'm not sure about tomorrow, we'll see." She smiled. Once again, her eyes did not. "C'mon, Tim, before we're both in trouble."

John leaned against the porch banister. "I'll keep my fingers crossed."

Carolyn nodded, turned away and started off at an easy jog.

Timmy hesitated. "Thanks, Johnny for bein' a buddy."

"Always. Say hi to your mom." He watched them race off into the distance and whispered, "Carolyn Parker, I would definitely like to see you again. Most definitely."

Thorns of the rose
Will often pierce the flesh
Of those with a gentle heart

Chapter Three
Nancy fights back

Clara Nelson stood on the opposite side of the table. She shook her head. "If you'd stop drawing on that cast and eat, your breakfast wouldn't be cold."

"Please ... heat it up just once more, then I'll gobble down every bit."

"The scrambled eggs will be like rubber. My land." Mrs. Nelson took Nancy's plate to the microwave, set it for forty-seconds, on medium and pressed start. "Cooking food in an electric box. I'll never get used to it."

Nancy colored in grey tips to the wing-feathers on the seagull she had drawn on her cast. "On *Star Trek* you just tell the computer to give you food an' it does."

"I suppose ...."

Nancy continued her art work and said, "Mom's here."

Mrs. Nelson stared through the door of the microwave half expecting the food inside to explode. "She's late. She'll be frantic."

"Mom's always frantic. She's an *A* personality—dedicated to her career." Nancy deepened the black of the seagull's eye and printed her initials just below the drawn bird's crooked feet.

"Child," said Clara. "How on earth do you learn such things?"

"From Sandy. She tells me all kinds of grown-up stuff."

The microwave beeped, Carolyn rushed in through the back door. "I'm late."

"Hi, Mom."

"Hi, honey. Any calls?"

Clara pulled the steaming eggs from the electric box. "Sandy called about twenty minutes ago."

Carolyn planted a kiss on top of her daughter's head. "How's the leg?"

"I can't feel a thing."

"All right, smarty--how does it look?"

Nancy backed her chair away from the table and pulled her robe aside. "If it spreads, I'll become a female *Corn creature* an' do a *mind-meld* with Mr. Spock."

Clara set the hot plate on the table. "Ms. Blair said Thomas Martin will be there at ten."

"Great ... I can't think of a worse person to spend the morning with." She grimaced at the yellowish, purple bruises on Nancy's upper-left thigh. The girl's *space-opera* comment was not too far fetched. Timmy's reference to the same TV show came to mind. *Two kids from two different worlds—they'd probably get along just great.* The only friends Nancy had were casual acquaintances from her therapy clinic. Carolyn wanted to keep it that way.

Nancy poked at her bruises. "Bet they'd hurt like hell to a normal kid."

Carolyn felt an icy stab deep in her heart. She shuddered. "I think Dr. Bailey would advise against what you're doing."

She pushed her fingers into the bruises, and said, "How big will they get?"

"They won't if you leave them alone. I'd rather you didn't become a *Gourd* anyway, and watch your mouth."

"Corn, Mother ... besides, I'm already an *alien* an' all my friends are freaks too!"

Another cut, deep inside. "That isn't true and you know it. We don't talk like that in this house."

"I think it--I think about it every single day." She raised her voice. "An' I dream about it every single night too!"

Clara wiped her hands on a dishtowel. "Oh, child ... don't be so angry."

"I'm not angry!"

Carolyn touched Nancy's shoulder. The girl jerked away, pushed the handle on her wheelchair, and raced toward the hall.

"Well, you're sure feeling sorry for yourself."

"I am not!" Her voice rose above the whirring of the chair's motor. "I'd just like to have friends who aren't screwed up!"

Carolyn's irritation held tears from coming. "Nancy Parker, you get right back in this kitchen and finish your breakfast."

"I won't!" The small voice echoed from the hallway. Nancy slammed her bedroom door.

Silence.

Carolyn spoke first. "I don't know what to do when she's like that."

Mrs. Nelson's voice cracked. "It just makes my heart ache to see that cast on her tiny arm." She put two pieces of bread in the toaster. "The poor child doesn't have enough problems, now she's bruised and broken on top of it ... and it's my doing."

"Clara. I don't want to hear that. I'll talk to Dr. Bailey Saturday. These mood-swings might have something to do with her medication."

The older woman put a box of *raisin bran* and a tub of soft spread on the table. "I don't want to speak out of turn, but I think part of the problem might be what she said."

Carolyn took off her headband and tossed her keys on the table. "Normal friends?"

"Yes."

"I hate that word."

"Carolyn, the girl never shares with anyone, other than us and a few of your friends, who aren't crippled."

Carolyn took a bowl down from the cupboard. "That word too. I hate it worse. You know my feelings on the subject. It's not open to debate. Nancy has friends and associates with people I choose."

Clara selected a spoon from the silverware drawer, confronting her friend and employer directly. "I'm sorry to say it, Carolyn, but you're hiding that child."

The younger woman looked away, stared out through the patio doors, across her upper-class, La Jolla beach property, to focus on a flock of gulls circling over the ocean. "I don't want to discuss it."

Carla fussed with the place setting, and continued. "I have to speak my mind, even if you get mad."

"Then say it. I'm late now, so what are a few more minutes?"

The gulls soared among themselves against the pale blue sky.

"You and Nancy are as close to me as

anyone in my own family. That little girl is the spice of my days. I think I know her pretty well. Hiding her isn't healthy."

"I'm not hiding her." Carolyn sat at the table, poured cereal into the bowl. "I'm protecting the kid from the shit-world I brought her into."

Clara pushed the bread-slices into the toaster, reset it to dark. "Your daughter is one of the most aware children I've ever known. The older she gets, the more aware she becomes." Clara took a carton of whole milk from the fridge and handed it to Carolyn. "The accident made me think about it more. A lot more. Nancy wants to relate to something—reach out to share. She disobeyed and put herself in danger so she could be close to the birds."

Carolyn poured milk and sprinkled two spoons of sugar over her bran flakes. "When the gazebo and the damn ramp are finished, that problem is history."

Clara Plucked the slices of hot toast from the toaster. She shook her head. "It isn't what you're doing for her, Carolyn, it's what you're *not* doing. The child's needs are growing as fast as she is."

Through a spoonful of cereal, Carolyn countered. "I provide everything Nancy needs and then some—what exactly is your point?"

Clara sliced the dry toast in half, just the way Carolyn liked it. "Dammit, Carolyn, I love you like a daughter and Nancy as if she were my own grandchild. Don't be so cold. Let the child into the world. She hasn't met one man you've dated."

"Business dates, Clara. That's all. Most of them are dip-shit clients I'm forced to deal with." Carolyn buttered a slice of toast, shaking her head. "What's that got to do with Nancy?"

Clara wiped her hands on her apron. "Seeing you in a relationship could make a difference for her."

"I don't have *relationships* I have neither the inclination nor the time."

"You should find the time."

"Thank you for the advice!" She bit off a chunk of dark toast. "Jesus! I got this same speech from Dr. Bailey last week. What the hell is this—reshape Carolyn month?"

Clara scraped Nancy's unfinished eggs into the disposal. "People who love you care about your life."

"Well, thank you both—I'll send you a card. God!"

Mrs. Nelson poured a cup of hot, black coffee, put it on the table in Carolyn's reach. "Maybe it's time Nancy made some new friends. You too."

"Thank you, Dr. Nelson, I'll think about it."

"Will you?"

Carolyn swallowed a sip of hot coffee and got up. "Clara, right now I need a quick shower and no more lecture. My child is mine. My life is mine. I think I'm doing quite well in both departments, thank you."

Clara stacked breakfast dishes in the left side of the double sink. "I've had my say. You'll hear no more of it. Are you mad?"

"Frustrated, yes. Mad, no. I even still kinda love you." Carolyn smiled.

"Do you still love me, Momma?"

Both women turned to see Nancy sitting in the hall, her chair facing the kitchen. Carolyn said, "Of course I love you. How long have you been there?"

"Long enough to hear you fighting."

"No, sweetheart." Carolyn put down her coffee cup. "We were talking, that's all."

Clara bit her lower lip and filled with emotion.

Carolyn flushed. "We weren't fighting, honey."

"You were angry, Mother."

"No, not angry."

"You were. Aunt Clara was almost crying."

Clara's voice broke as she spoke. "No, child, I was just concerned about you, that's all--"

“You were about to cry—an’ Mom was angry!” Nancy studied both women for a moment.

"I've seen your *dip-shit* dates, Mom. They're nowhere near good enough for you."

"Nancy!"

"It's true, Mom." The child moved her chair further into the kitchen area. "You can do better and you know it. You *are* hiding me. I hate it!" Nancy's eyes flooded with tears. "Aunt Clara's right — you're wrong!" The child pounded the arms of her wheelchair. "I want to meet somebody new. Somebody who isn't twisted an' sick an' crippled and hurt. Somebody who can stand up and walk—even run! Somebody who can help me with my chair and feed the birds with me! I'm sick of crippled kids! I'm sick of being a cripple!"

Clara sat down at the table, and cried into her apron.

Carolyn had words that would not come. The ache in her heart became the pain of her daughter's truth.

Weep not for yourself.
Be gracious and
compassionate,
slow to anger and
rich in love.
Reach out to the
afflicted children.

Chapter Four
A call from home

The phone rang just as John finished shaving. He switched off the razor, grabbed the phone off the toilet lid and sat down. "John in the john, an' I'm runnin' late, Bob."

It wasn't his boss.

"What'd you say, Son?" It was his mother, Sarah, calling from Texas.

"Nothing, Ma--How's everything in Huntsville?"

"Fine, Sonny, just fine. You know how beautiful it gets here in the spring. Nice an' green. Not brown like California."

"Great, Ma. So what's wrong?" He waited to hear bad news.

"Does something have to be wrong for a mother to call her son long distance?"

No. it doesn't, but that's what it usually means. And yes. I know how great it is in Huntsville: boring, muggy and boring. That's how it always is in get-down, kick-ass-Huntsville. "I guess not. I just haven't heard from you in a while." He rolled his eyes, shook his head.

"Johnny, it's you who forgot how to write and use the phone." She spoke loud. She always did on the telephone. Sarah believed the farther away the party was, the louder she had to talk.

"I haven't had any news really, and I've been busy." He glanced at his watch on the sink.

"Hello. This is your son. How are you? That's news enough for and old mother all alone in a big house. What's that, eight seconds? Call collect if you can't afford it. You can't be too busy to talk to your mother for eight seconds, Johnny."

He took a deep breath, held it, closed his eyes, leaned his head back against the wall. "Let's not do this, Ma, please. Every time you call we get into the same game. Not today okay?" He opened his eyes and stared at the ceiling. John pictured his mother seated on the black stool by the phone. That ever-present chrome one with two pull-out steps and it's adjustable backrest. The very one he had used to snitch cookies from the third shelf of the cupboard.

Sarah would be leaning on the end of the counter looking bright and fresh in her lemon yellow kitchen which was Kept as spotless as an operating room. On the table he imagined an assortment of flowers, cut that morning and arranged neatly in a heavy crystal vase perfectly centered on a diamond-shaped blue cloth with white fringe.

"It's a game now for a lonely mother to care about her son's welfare?" Sarah's voice fluttered.

"No, Ma, that's not what I meant." He paused, took another breath and checked his watch again. "Are there flowers on the table?"

"Yes." Her tone brightened. "I cut them just before I called, why?"

"Nothing, I just remember your daily flowers that's all." He sat forward, elbows on his knees. "I wish we got along better. I really do." He stared at the small rug under his feet wondering when it was last cleaned.

"There's a lot of your father in you, Sonny, but you're really a good boy."

A long silence.

"Thanks. Look, I have to get ready for work. I'll write a letter this weekend."

"Letter, schmetter! I want you to come home for your birthday. You said you'd try. And don't lie to your mother. I should have a heart attack if I got a letter from you next week." Sarah's voice shook.

"Trying and doing are two different things. If I get the time off, I'll come home. That's all I can tell you. See, Ma. We yell every time we talk to each other." John shook his head and got up to turn on the shower.

"Come home. We'll yell face-to-face." She caught her breath and lowered her voice. "I would be very happy if you came home, Sonny."

"I'll talk to my boss today, then it's his call." John tested the water and twisted on more cold.

"Good. How are your studies?" For Sarah, the die was cast. Her son *would* be home for his birthday.

"I'm doing well." He checked the time again.

"What about you and Chris?"

"Don't start on that, Ma!"

"I'm hoping, Sonny. If you tried you could work it out." Sarah wouldn't let go of it if she lived to be a hundred.

"We're divorced! Chris is history! That's that. Drop it, okay?" He squeezed his eyes shut, trying to cut off the memory of the scattered pieces of a marriage he wanted to work. *I love you.* Christine's voice slammed against the back wall of his brain. *Can it always be like this?* Her words echoed off the feelings of a dream destroyed. A dream that chased him into a pit of depression more times than he cared to recall.

We'll never stop loving, John, I promise. The words twisted into pointed shapes and tore into his heart, ending, as always, in distortion and ache. When Christine's love stopped, it cut John to ribbons.

"Just remember, Sonny, your father and I stayed together, God rest his soul, because we took holy vows. That's something your generation doesn't care about."

"Ma, I heard this all before. Now, I have to go." He spoke in quiet, even tones and concentrated on the water rushing onto the floor of the shower stall. The fragments of Christine's memory dissipated into the steam.

"All right, son. The party's all planned. Some old friends are coming. It'll be good for you." Sarah was as sure of herself as she could ever be. After all, her boy couldn't disappoint his mother.

"I'm not sure I'll get the time off. Why don't we just wait an' see?" He held his hand under the shower then ran it over his face.

"Don't worry about that, sonny. I got faith. Something you should have more of." Sarah Freeman would stick to that platform until hell froze over.

"Okay, I'll call as soon as I know." He stared at his image in the mirror. Steam fogged out all detail. Like the picture he had of himself in his mind, blurred, without definition.

"I'll be waiting, Son. God bless you." Sarah smiled and kissed the phone as she always had since he could remember.

"Take care, Ma." He put the receiver down. A shudder ran through him. Guilt for not being closer to his mother, for his broken marriage and for not having his lousy act together.

He took off his trunks and socks, got into the shower. He thought of Carolyn again.

* * * *

Asking for time off occupied John's mind as he drove through the golden morning toward the University of California, San Diego, where Professor Robert Lawrence and the track team waited. He assisted professor Lawrence on a student-teacher program through the University's athletic department and was being considered for a full time position.

John existed on an endowment from his father's investments and a living allowance provided by Uncle Sam. If he maintained his grade average, and satisfied the requirements of student-teaching, he would have a great future. It was his first *real* opportunity since leaving Huntsville. He had trouble making the necessary commitment.

He pulled his faded VW into a permit parking

lot near an outdoor running track. After passing several rows of cars he found a spot. He grabbed his bag, climbed out of the car and jogged toward a distant set of bleachers.

Professor Lawrence was sitting three rows up. He checked his watch as he caught sight of John running up the path toward the track.

The professor taught Philosophy at the University and assisted the Athletic Director during the summer schedule. His forty-seven years were hidden in the mass of his tall, wel1-conditioned frame. Dr. Lawrence had taken John under his wing and his evaluation would make or break the full time job. He leaned forward smiled, and caught the stopwatch swinging around the neck of his blue sweat suit. "Morning!"

"Sorry I'm late." John's words bounced out as he reached the foot of the bleachers. He bent forward puffing, and dropped his bag on the lowest bench. "My mother called while I was trying to get ready." He straightened and took a deep breath of the morning.

Professor Lawrence stepped down beside his pupil and patted him on the shoulder. "How's your mother doing?" He grabbed John's bag and handed it to him as they started waking along the edge of the track.

“She's depressed again, and wants me

home for my birthday." He glanced at the professor, then at the ground. They walked in step.

"That's what you wanted to see me about?" Dr. Lawrence looked straight ahead.

John noted Robert's face, there wasn't any change of expression. His ever-present smile held fast. *I admire this man. He's gone to bat for me, and here I am, ready to bug-out on him when I'm needed most.*

At least ten-seconds passed before John answered. "Yeah, basically ...."

The professor looked at John with a degree of question. "I don't see any problem with a few days off for your birthday." He took an enjoyable, deep breath. "I love spring mornings up here."

"I need a month, Bob. Not just a day or two." They stopped walking.

Dr. Lawrence checked the time again. "What's the problem?" His face did change then, to an expression of concern.

"My head's screwed up. I have to sort things out. I'm not sure I want to teach. I just need time." He looked away, unable to meet the professor's eyes.

"Okay. It's a long time to be off your program, but we'll work it out." He looked at John for a moment and put his arm over his shoulder.

"Let's sit for a minute." Professor Lawrence stepped in and sat on the second level of bleachers.

John sat below him. "Maybe teaching isn't right for me. I'm not sure. I'm not really sure of anything." He set his bag down and rubbed his face with both hands, then looked up at Dr. Lawrence.

"I'd like to do what's right for you." The professor tasted the air again. "I've been where you are. I think I know what you're going through." He looked into John's eyes with concern and put a strong hand on his shoulder. "Getting the Athletic Director to turn you loose for a month could be tough." He blinked, let out a breath and gripped John's shoulder again. "I'll try, but remember, I'm just an assistant, not the boss." He smiled and shook him gently.

John grinned, and looked out across the empty field. "Thanks" He couldn't find words just then.

"How old are you, thirty-four-thirty-five?"

"I'll be thirty-six this month, why?" John continued staring into space.

"Isn't it time you had some idea where your life is headed?" Dr. Lawrence pulled his hand off John's shoulder and checked the time again.

“Right, I should, but I'm afraid of it.” He

turned to meet the professor's eyes.

"Don't be. Decide what's right for you and go for it." Dr. Lawrence saw ache creep over John's face and set his expression to doubt.

"I had it together. Then the shit hit the fan." He looked away.

A group of summer-students walked slowly toward the campus library, books in bundles carried at their chests. They laughed and talked of a weekend past and another to come. Cares of the world hadn't reached them yet. They were protected. He wasn't.

"Work at what you have here. "Your grade average is up and your student-teacher progress is excellent."

"I've heard this speech before." John folded his arms across his knees. "I'm doing great. I got it made, right?" His tone was more frustration than anger, but it was sharp.

"Right! Now follow through." He raised his voice to match John's. "Don't let things fall apart this time. The older you get, the harder it is to put things back together. Think about it." The professor stood "Let's get inside and make sure the team's ready." He stepped down off the bleachers and stopped in front of John. "Are you coming or would you like today off too?" He laughed and slapped him on the arm.

John glanced up at the professor. *I owe*

This guy a lot, he thought, and smiled. "What about the time off?"

"I'll talk to the boss this afternoon. It'll take time to get somebody, but I'm sure we can work it out."

"Thanks Bob. I knew I could count on you." John stood and brushed off the back of his pants.

"Can I count on you? If I didn't think you had a future here, I wouldn't be training you. I hope I'm not wasting my time." Lawrence looked at John, waiting for a positive response.

"When I get back, I'll have your answer. That's a promise." He smacked the Professor on the arm and they jogged off the field.

* * * *

John's thoughts filled with Carolyn. Her warm voice danced through his mind. So did the promise he made to Timmy. The Sunday ball game. *I will be there.*

Soft spring rain brings
the promise of change.

Every new rose
will bear fresh thorns.

Chapter Five
For Nancy's sake

Carolyn pulled into her private spot in the parking lot of the ten-story PRC building, cut the engine of her Mercedes. She sat for a moment, gathering strength to face a morning with Thomas Martin. *What are a few hours? Martin's a major player. Brooks & Associates needs the business. Forget the fact that he's a royal pain in the ass.*

She was Marketing V/P for radio and TV. and put up with him because he's important to the agency. "Yeah--right," she mumbled. "I'll take his crap for Nancy's sake—for her, for me and the agency."

Five minutes later, Carolyn entered the lobby of the ad agency's second floor offices.

Jenny, the receptionist, adjusted her headset and waved. “Mr. Brooks is in conference, may I take a message?” She held up a hand to Carolyn. "What company are you with Mr. Spencer? Cyteck. I'll tell Mr. Brooks you called." To Carolyn she said, "Martin's in your conference room and he's drooling as usual."

"Great." She plucked her messages from the plastic holder on the counter. "Any voice mail?"

"Three in the last hour."

"I'll face Martin first."

"Good luck."

"Thanks."

"There's a fresh pot of coffee waiting."

"You're an angel, Jen."

"My husband thinks so, but he'd rather have me as a devil."

"Right, thanks for sharing."

Thomas Martin was on the phone in Carolyn's conference room. He waved at her and concluded his call. "I don't give a damn what Harry says. Nothing goes until I say the word. Understand?" He winked at Carolyn. "I'll be there by noon. Nothing happens till then." He hung up. "You're late."

"And you're early. "Let me get some coffee."

"The early bird gets you-know-what."

Stuck with you, she thought. "Can I warm your cup?"

"Carolyn, you can warm anything I have any time you're ready" He grinned, sat back and watched her walk to the far side of the conference room.

You're a scum-bag, Martin. The only warm thing I'll ever give you is spit in the eye. She smiled and fetched the coffee pot from the machine near the wet bar. "Sandy says you're ready to go to TV."

"You got it, babe, and I want you in charge of the production."

Carolyn came back to the conference table and poured fresh coffee into Martin's cup. "What's the concept?"

"I want you to help me with that. We'll have to spend some time together to get it right. I think we'll have to do some overtime on the project." He touched her wrist as she filled a cup for herself.

She shuddered. "I can find special time if you need it." She gripped the handle of the coffee pot much harder than necessary.

Martin grinned. "Not here. At my place. I don't want phones and other crap involved. Just you an' me, alone, so we can concentrate on the project together."

She carried the pot back to the service bar. "It's easier here." *Don't hold your breath.* She gritted her teeth. "I'll set up whatever you need."

Sandy had pulled Martin's file earlier and clipped a *smiley* face to the cover and set it by the coffee machine.

Carolyn brought the folder to the conference table and sat across from him. "What are you thinking of in terms of budget for this project?"

"Fifty *K* give or take." He smiled, slid his foot under the table until it touched Carolyn's right pump. He stared at her over the rim of his cup, "As I said, I want you in complete charge." He winked again. "Your commission would be quite substantial."

The look in his eyes burned through her very existence. *You, Mr. Martin, are a piece of dog shit.* She nodded and said, "Sixty-five-thousand would give you a good, slick production. You might consider raising the budget."

"I love it when you deal. I love it. It turns me on. What about you an' me working closely on this?"

You make me want to puke. That was her thought. She said, with a careful smile, "If it takes extra hours, we'll find a way to get it done, but remember, overtime adds to your cost."

"You're worth every dime." He grinned and sat back.

"The agency will meet your needs, Mr. Martin, whatever it takes."

"Can we discuss my needs over dinner?"

"We can, if Mr. Brooks approves and joins us to cut the deal."

"I was thinking of dinner for two."

Carolyn shivered and held her temper. She flashed a corporate smile. "I can't approve anything without Mr. Brooks' okay. If you want it done during a business dinner, I'm sure he'd be more than willing to join us." In her heart she said, *I wouldn't be seen with you, alone, outside this office ever.*

"Set it up." He sipped more coffee. "I want a twenty-six-week run on this project and I demand your best people."

"You'll get the best we can give."

"I'd like that very much, and you can call me Tom." He drained his cup and stared at her.

She felt his lust sift through her heart. She remembered Alan Tagart and how he dragged her down. *A piq, that's what you are, Martin. A fat pig.*

* * * *

The memory took her back eleven years

* * * *

Alan's face broke away from the back of her mind and hung in front of her. The image glared, dripping sweat and wasted.

Sex, drugs, and rock and roll.

Make it happen again, Alan ... take me over

the top. And so he did.

Reality came crashing back when Carolyn knew she was pregnant.

Alan split for new highs.

Eleven years, and the anger remained. An image of Alan's wet face formed over the grinning countenance of Thomas Martin. She hated both men at that moment and it filled her with bitter contempt.

He said, "It could mean a great deal to you if you play my game."

Before she could stop it rage shot up from the pit of her stomach and burst out. "Game! Is that what this is? I thought we were talking about a television campaign." Her throat went chalk-dry. "I don't play games, Mr. Martin!" She pushed away from the table.

He shivered. Very few ever raised their voice to him. "I meant the campaign."

"I know what you meant!" Carolyn drew her fury back in a deep breath and forced a chilling smile.

Silence.

Stephen Brooks came in and glanced from Carolyn to Martin. The room was so full of sparks he could almost smell ozone. "Hi," he said. "Everything under control?"

Carolyn stood rigid, gripped the back of her chair. "It is now."

"Great." Steve shook Martin's hand. "I got tied up. Mind if I get in on the concept?"

Martin's cold stare caught Carolyn's eyes. "Not at all, I think the *three* of us need to work on this project."

Steve sat down. "I have no problem with that."

Carolyn walked to the service bar. "I was just telling Mr. Martin we're a team and we'll play the *game* to the max."

Steve chuckled. "Count on it, Tom."

Carolyn poured fresh water into the coffee maker. A sudden image of John Freeman and Timmy came to mind. For an instant she could see them together with Nancy. *I don't need the hassle.* She shook the thought away.

Chapter Six
“Cut! That’s a wrap.”

PARAMOUNT STUDIOS - STAGE 27:

"Places everybody, this is take five." The assistant director clicked off his bullhorn, turned to a group of extras. "You, in the blue jacket."

Alan nodded. "Tagart."

"I couldn't give a damn what your name is. When Mr. Stevens calls *action* you count to five. Not four, not six, just five—got it?"

"Yeah, five."

"I'm impressed. Everybody else had it but you."

"I just thought."

"Please, try not to. We're doing this take *because* you thought. Again, on five, you cross the set between Ms. Montgomery and Mr. Lewis, pause two beats, react to the gun without dialogue. We don't need an extra adding lines."

Alan sneered. "Oh shit! Seemed appropriate at the time."

"Look, I'm being cool here. You're in on a pass, dude. You got a teeny, tiny break to be in a strong scene. Step over the line just once more an' you're off the lot."

A harsh bell rang. The A/D clicked on his bull horn.

"Stand by. Light it." He glanced at Alan. "On five you move, see the gun, count two beats, keep your mouth shut and get out of the shot."

"No problem, man."

"There better not be." Into the bull horn he shouted, "Let's have slate."

The cameraman yelled, "Speed."

The director, George Stevens, Jr. said, "Settle down ... and *action!*"

On the count of five, Alan crossed the set between Elizabeth Montgomery and Jeffrey Lewis, paused, reacted to the gun and shouted, "Son-of-a-bitch!" He ran out of the shot.

Stevens yelled, "Cut! That's a wrap." He grabbed the A/D's bull horn. "You in the blue, would you come over here please?"

Alan grinned at the other extras that were shaking their heads. “Yes, sir.” He walked up to the camera crew and stuck out his hand to the director. “Mr. Stevens, I’m Alan Tagart.”

Stevens smiled. He pumped Alan's hand. "Mr. Tagart, I'm glad to know you. That was quite a performance."

"Thanks."

The A/D clenched his teeth and glared at Alan. "You just had your moment of fame."

Stevens held up his hand. "Judy."

The script girl came over. "Would you be kind enough to take down Mr. Tagart's name and guild card number?"

Alan beamed from ear-to-ear. He spelled his name and gave the woman his Extras' Guild number. "That's one 'g' in Tagart and the number is 656347."

Stevens said, "Put Mr. Tagart in my general and personal file right away."

The assistant director chuckled.

Alan said, "You're gonna use my line right?"

Stevens smiled, handed the A/D the horn. "The non-written dialogue cuts him a better check I think. Doesn't it, Ray?"

He nodded. "Close to fifty bucks more."

Alan shook his head. "God, I died an' went to heaven. Your old man directed *SHANE.* Jesus!"

"Yes, my father directed *SHANE* and there were a lot of extras on location who followed instructions to the letter. Stevens reclined in his

Canvas chair behind the camera. "None of them acted like you just did."

Alan thrust his hands in his pockets and winked at the assistant director. "Incredible, man. *Shane.* I saw that flick at least seventeen times, it was a blast. It shook me, I mean to the core. I remember Jack's line ... Jack Palance. He said, *'You're a low down Yankee liar.'* Then the little guy, what's his name?"

Stevens said, "Elijah Cook."

"Yeah him. He went for his gun an' *BAM!* Jack cleared leather and Cook was history. That scene changed westerns forever. I'll never forget the echo of the gunshot after Jack fired."

The director got off his chair and shook Alan's hand. "And you're history, Mr. Tagart. Your little adlib-line won't appear in my film. You won't get paid for it, and no one will ever hear it. You're an ass, Mr. Tagart. If I can do it, and I think I can, I'll have you banned from the lot. Now get off my set!"

Alan sucked a breath and swallowed hard. He glanced at the A/D. "I'm sorry, Mr. Stevens, I didn't mean any harm."

The assistant director grabbed Alan's shoulder. "Your outta here."

Tagart pulled away. "Lewis blew his line. That's what's pissing you off?"

Ray said, “Hit the street, asshole!”

Alan tore off his blue jacket. "Fuck you, Ray! An' you too, Stevens!"

Two other extras grabbed Alan, pulled him back. One of them said, "Shut your mouth, Tagart." They walked him off the set, out of the sound stage and straight to the parking area.

Bill Ferris, who got Alan into the extra's union, shook his head and cranked up his Toyota. "Man you blew it. You just threw it away. What the hell's in your head?"

"That A/D pissed me off. Who the fuck *is* he?"

"You're on self-destruct. Ray's important, man. Jesus! I get you in and you turn it to shit."

"My line added, man."

"The line sucked. It didn't belong! Goddammit, you cost Stevens three, four, maybe five thousand dollar retakes. The guild's gonna hear about this."

"Fuck the shit-ass union. I don't need it."

"To work in this town—you damn well need it!" Ferris hit the freeway and was immediately bogged down in heavy traffic. "I think we can get something in San Diego if you can keep your cool an' work a few TV spots."

Alan twisted the ends of a fresh joint and ran the toke under his nose. "Do I get lines?"

"Who do you think you are, Anthony Quinn? You'll get a gig and a paycheck. All you have to do is show your great face, shake your ass, and maybe suck on a beer. Who gives a shit? Mellow out. I can hook you up with Brooks. It's big-time commercial stuff."

"TV ads, man?"

Ferris braked the Toyota in a sea of red taillights. "Friggin' traffic. Christ on a surfboard. Yeah, I do spots for the agency. Carolyn Parker's my contact. She's a great lady. I've done more than a dozen spots for her already. Car stuff, waterbed commercials, furniture, you name it."

Alan sat forward and lit his toke. "Carolyn Parker?"

Ferris smacked the steering wheel. "Damn yo-yos. Yeah, Carolyn Parker. She's sharp and good to look at."

Alan grinned. "We go to San Diego on Monday."

"Fine with me, but if there ain't no lines don't add any."

"Hell with lines. Get us out of this traffic. I want some food. We'll hang out till Monday. Then we go to San Diego."

"Sounds good." He glanced at his buddy. "No dope on the way, got it?"

"Okay, no prob, man." Alan sucked on his joint and yelled, "Cut! That's a wrap!" They both laughed.

The prick of the thorn
belies the beauty of
the rose.

Something wicked
This way comes.

Chapter Seven
Necessary Encounter

EARLIER THAT SAME FRIDAY MORNING:

John smiled and waved at other runners as he headed north along the beach. *They should be around here somewhere.* He passed a group of sandpipers dancing in and out of receding waves, poking their needle-beaks into the wet sand. Seeing Carolyn again was on John's mind along with the possibility of getting the time off he needed.

Decide what you want, and go for it. The words of Professor Lawrence crossed the image of Carolyn as John eased his pace.

Carolyn.

Just looking at her tells you she's above your class. He adjusted his headband to keep hair out of his eyes and continued scanning the beach for Timmy.

The bank of morning fog had drifted out to sea, leaving the beach drying in the sun. *Exposed; unprotected. The thought cut into a sensitive corner of John's memory.*

Christine. Broken dreams.

He shook his head. A pricking-cold chill raced up his spine and ran across the back of his neck. He tried to balance the scales in his heart. The side with hurt won. *Sure. Go for it.*

Carolyn. Right.

Open yourself up to more of the same bullshit. That's just what you need. Another screwing over while you're trying to get your life together.

He caught sight of them in the distance and grinned. The chill melted away as quickly as a dusting of early April snow.

"Timmy." John's voice rose into the wind and carried above the roaring surf. "Hey, Timmy," he yelled again.

Carolyn and her young friend turned to see John waving and running toward them. She pushed a lock of hair away from her face, waved and managed a slight smile. "Hi," she said.

John came closer. Carolyn's expression stiffened. "We didn't expect to see you." She met his eyes for a moment and then turned away.

Timmy shouted, "Carolyn's got a big

meeting an' we're quitting early." He glanced from one adult to the other, delighted to share such grown-up friendship.

"Okay. Let's run back to your car." John sensed coolness from Carolyn.

"All Right!" Timmy blurted. "I'll beat you both!" The boy headed north, kicking up sand as he ran.

"You ready for it?" John chuckled, suppressing a clear feeling of rejection.

"Why not?" Her eyes met John's and pulled away. She ran after the boy as if she were afraid to be alone with the man.

He chased after her thinking, *Yesterday she was open, today she's locked up tight.* He caught up with her in a few strides and adjusted his pace to match hers. "I'll have to get up earlier to run with you guys." His words came out clumsy. He tried to recover and land on his feet. "So, how long will you be running here?"

She turned toward him with a hint of question in her eyes. "Through the rest of the weekend, why?" Her shining auburn ponytail bounced back and forth as she ran.

"I just thought it might be fun to share the time with Timmy."

Keep at it. John thought. *You're a shoo-in for jerk of the year.*

They ran for several yards before Carolyn

responded. "With Timmy and *me,* right?" Her smile was cold. She fell back to a fast walk near a parking lot.

"And share the time with you too." A thought crashed into his head. *Don't make a fool of yourself. Step easy. This lady has class.* The suggestion rattled through his brain like nails being dumped onto a tin tray.

Carolyn stopped short. She stared at him through eyes that had grown distant. Her face looked cold.

He ignored the voice of his better judgment and asked the question that found itself on the tip of his tongue. "How about going to Timmy's game Sunday and maybe dinner after?"

The softer look returned, but her eyes remained distant. "I can't." she stared straight ahead.

"I just thought it might be good for the kid with both of us there." John's voice wavered while his ego added an option, "Maybe some other time."

"I really don't have time for socializing right now." She looked at him and grinned. "Thanks anyway," she added, then shifted her eyes away.

She's turning me down altogether. He didn't handle rejection well. *Maybe I should keep my mouth shut. There might be a chance,* he thought, but didn't. "Where do you usually run?" Another pause before she answered.

"In La Jolla ... near my beach house."

They approached the parking lot where Timmy was waiting.

"I beat you guys by a mile!" He leaned against the front fender of a black Mercedes. "You're tired, Miss. May I offer you a ride in my new car?" The boy animated a bow and added, "The very best for such a fine lady."

"You'll get a ride on the foot of the guy who owns that car if he sees you leaning on it." He and Carolyn came to the edge of the parking lot.

"I'm the guy," she said. "I don't mind at all." She pulled a set of keys from her running shorts, glanced toward John, and tossed the keys to Timmy. "Would you get our towels please?"

"I'm sorry. It was my mistake."

"Why would a high-priced car fluster you so much?" Her brown eyes darkened. "Or is the fact that I own it the problem?" She cocked her head, eyes flashing like fire in the sun.

"No! It's not that, it's—"

"I suppose not. No. It's what I hear from men everyday." She raised her voice. "Nice car—did your husband get a good deal? Great house—is your man in real estate?" Her breasts rose as she drew a deep breath. "I'll bet she did a lot of bed-hopping on her way to that job." Her hard swallow caused a flutter in her voice. "Those cracks I hear secondhand because the male assholes that make them haven't got the guts to say them to my face!"

Timmy climbed out of the car looking concerned. "What's wrong?" He glanced from one to the other.

"Nothing." Carolyn relaxed a little, and glared at John. "Nothing I didn't expect anyway."

"I'm sorry. I didn't mean to insult you."

"You really don't get it, do you?" Carolyn yanked the towel from around her neck and blotted her face.

"No, I'm afraid I don't." He moved closer.

She stepped back and handed her towel to Timmy. "Your male ego, Mr. Freeman, wouldn't let macho logic connect me, a woman, with an expensive Mercedes. You assumed the car belonged to a *man*."

The woman sounds like a stone bitch. I know better. Dammit—somehow, I know she's not really that way. "My reaction to you and the car meant nothing." He hesitated. "I don't care what car you drive, where your house is, or how much it cost. He watched the bitter anger twist her face. *There's more going on here than a loose comment about her damn Benz.*

John walked toward the car and stopped at the edge of the parking lot. He ran his hands through his hair and smiled at Timmy. "You okay, champ?"

"I hate fighting." He turned away and stared at the ocean. “Right before my dad left, he and my mom yelled and screamed at each other every day. They scared my little sister and she hid in her room shaking and crying. They called each other names. The day my dad left, he hit mom and hurt her. I tried to help her an’ he came after me.”

John put his arm around the boy. “That wasn’t really your father, Tim. It was his frustration and anger making him act that way.”

Tim turned and hugged his man-friend. “I don’t want you guys to be fighting—please don’t fight.”

Carolyn knelt beside the boy and wiped tears from his face. “We’re not fighting, we just disagree right now.” She looked up at John. “Sometimes adults aren’t too smart.”

Tim pulled away. “What about Sunday’s ballgame?” He studied their faces. “Will you both come?”

John ruffled Timmy’s hair. “I’ll be right

behind home plate. Count on it."

Carolyn wiped her face with the towel. "I can't be sure, but I'll try."

"Please be there, both of you." He paused. "I gotta go. I have to help get my sister ready for school."

The boy studied his friends a moment, turned and ran south.

"Timmy!" Carolyn's voice rose into the wind. "I'll drive you." Her words were lost, carried away in the crashing surf.

The boy disappeared into scattered groups of people enjoying the morning.

"We both drove him," mumbled John, thinking out loud.

"What did we do?" Carolyn looked away and got into the car.

"We drove Timmy away with our stupid little scene." He closed the car door and leaned toward the open window.

Carolyn started the engine. She held the steering wheel with both hands and looked straight ahead. "Our exchange was *your* doing, not mine." She released the brake and slipped the Mercedes into reverse.

"Fault in this case is the least of the issue." He placed his hands on the door frame bringing him closer to Carolyn. *She's beautiful, why is she so hostile?* Another door slammed open in the back of his mind and out came bits and pieces of a long-forgotten evening. It was John's first meeting with Christine, his ex-wife. Actually, it was more of an encounter than a meeting. She too was beautiful, opinionated, and more than a little pissed-off at men in general.

* * * *

He had gone to a half-planned party on a friends invitation. By the time he approached Christine, he was crocked. They argued about something. Neither of them could ever remember the specific details of their disagreement. It hadn't mattered at the time and it didn't matter in the end.

The marriage lasted just under four years and ended badly.

John changed after the divorce, he mellowed.

Christine didn't.

* * * *

"I don't have time to discuss it," said Carolyn. "It's not that important anyway." She turned and looked at him.

"It's important to Timmy." John raised his voice again and stepped back from the car.

"You've known him, what, an hour longer than you've known me?"

Carolyn took her foot off the brake and the car moved backward. "I've become his friend in that length of time and learned to dislike you in less. Now, if you'll excuse me, I have to go." The car rolled faster as she backed it out of the parking spot.

"Wait a minute!" John moved along with the car. "The kid's life has been turned upside down by his parents' divorce. The last memories he has of his mom and dad together are full of fighting and bitter hate."

Carolyn kept backing the car and John moved along with it. "He obviously got some childish idea that putting us together would cover part of the ugliness and give him something nice to hang on to."

Carolyn stopped the car and stared at him. "What is it you do for a living, Mr. Freeman?"

"I'm an instructor at UCSD."

"Psychology?"

"No, athletics."

"I'm relieved. Stick to sweat socks and gym trunks. You make a lousy counselor."

"You know, Carolyn, with a little more practice, you could become a real professional bitch!" He glared at her.

“Thanks. I work very hard to achieve that

goal." She dropped the car into gear and shot forward.

"I still want to take you out anyway."

"Not a chance, Mr. Freeman." Carolyn shouted, "I deal with macho, male egos every day. I don't need them in my private life." The Mercedes left the parking lot and headed into traffic.

John stood on the edge of blacktop. *How could a great day turn to shit so fast?*

Clip the rose from
Its bush.
Avoid the prick of its
sharp thorns.

Chapter Eight
Open Wounds

The rear screen door slammed shut and startled Janet. She stood in the kitchen fixing sandwiches to take to work, and for Tim's lunch."

Do you have to slam that door?"

Timmy went straight to his room. "I'm talking to you." The boy didn't respond. Janet Collins stuffed her son's tuna sandwich in a plastic bag and shoved hers in a small, paper sack. "I swear to God."

Morning sun spilled into the front of the house from large east windows facing the street. Warm light spread across dark oak flooring leading from the extra-large entrance way and onto plush gray living room carpet. That elegantly designed entrance was the main reason Janet fell in love with the place on sight. None of that meant anything to her now.

"You're in trouble, young man." Her words

sounded harsh and edgy. She walked down the hall.

What little dust could be found in the house rose like tiny flakes of snow in the rays of sun when she passed through.

She knocked on Timmy's door, "You're making me mad." A moment passed. She tapped again.

The door opened. "Sorry I'm late, Mom." He went across the room, pulling off his sweat shirt.

"I had to get Beth ready without your help. That means giving her a bath, making breakfast, doing lunches, and putting myself together on top of it." Janet tightened her robe and glanced in the mirror behind Timmy to check her hair. She never needed much makeup or hair fixing. She had a quiet, soft attractiveness. "I barely got her on the bus in time. Why are you late?"

The boy turned to face his mother through burning, tear-filled eyes. "How come adults fight so easy?" Pain welled up inside and wrenched his heart.

"What happened?" Janet went to her son. "Did your friend say something wrong?"

Timmy flopped into the chair by his desk. "No. Not to me ... I don't know what went crazy, but it sure did—a lot." He turned away.

Janet knelt beside him and put her slender arm over his shoulder. "Tell me what happened." She pushed a lock of hair away from his eyes and kissed him on the forehead.

"I'm not sure ...." He rested his head against her chest. "They don't like each other, Mom ... an' I wanted them to—real bad." Timmy cried into his mother's robe.

"Who fought? Tell me who you're talking about." She hugged the boy. A stab of old pain pricked the thin shell of her heart. *Fighting? Yes, fighting.* The coarse meaning of the words raked through her.

Timmy pulled himself away and fumbled through a pile of baseball cards, two or three soiled sweat shirts and a couple of empty Diet Pepsi cans, for a Kleenex. The tissue was found in a battered box under the mom-maddening mess, which covered his desk. Janet shook her head. It wasn't a good moment to scold for lack of neatness.

Tim wiped his eyes and blew his nose. "I'm talking about my friend, Johnny—the guy I run with." He plucked another tissue out of the box and took a deep breath. "I've been working out with Johnny for a while and he tells me all the time about how having somebody to share with is so darn important."

A shudder ran through Janet. The words touched the back of her neck with sharp, icy fingers.

"So, the other day, I met this lady, Carolyn, and I guess I kinda got them together ...." He struggled to hide his hurt. "This morning—on the beach," he continued in a shaking voice, "just a day after they met ... they fought." The words came hard. "Why do older people fight?" He fetched a short breath. "Why, Mom?"

Janet reached out and took the boy to her breast again. She saw the hazy vision of the boy's father throwing up angry words. She shivered at the memory of the horror-mask painted on the man's face. "It's never easy to explain, Tim ... people, grown-ups, say things." Janet wanted to say something more. She reached deep inside to assemble a statement worth the telling. Her son was about to hear a truth—a reality he would not fully understand for years. "Your friends argued—"

"They were mad at each other, Mom—really mad." Timmy interrupted in uneven words muffled against Janet's chest.

"Okay ... they fought." She tried to quiet her own sorrow. "Carolyn and Johnny disagreed because something between them is wrong." Janet hugged her son harder to get the strength she needed to find the words and put them right. "Timmy, your friends touched something very deep—right away." She swallowed an ache like copper shavings that seemed on fire as they went down. "If only your father and I had expressed our feelings openly in the beginning." *If only we had.* An old drawer, bursting with yesterdays, blew open in a shadowed corner of her mind. "If we could've done that, things would be different." The mother—the woman—the heart-broken, impressionable young lady from Nebraska, pressed her face into the back of her son's innocent neck.

"What's so good about fighting?" Timmy wrenched as he mumbled the comment against his mother. "You an' dad screamed and he's gone now!"

Janet pulled her arms tighter around the boy squeezing out a sigh. "We did ... we yelled—oh, how we blasted back and forth." Tears burned and ran down her cheeks. "You heard the roaring. God forgive us. The bitterness was vile." She opened her eyes. "We fought too late." She felt old wounds leaking fresh blood. "Carolyn and John have a chance—do you see that?"

The boy let out a breath, sniffed and pulled away. "No! I don't." He shook his head and wiped his hand under his nose. "How can being mad at someone make it okay?"

She got up and took two tissues from the box. "When your father and I started the yelling we were picking at old sores." She blew her nose and sat on the edge of Tim's unmade bed. "The trouble came from disappointments and anger that happened years before."

Timmy looked at his mother then sat beside her. "How, Mom? I don't know what you mean." He leaned against Janet's shoulder and finished wiping the wetness off his face.

She smiled and brushed her hand through his tousled hair. "You feel better now because we talked don't you?"

The boy searched his mother's face for a moment and watched his reflection in her bright, green eyes. "I guess so ... some."

"That's what I mean, Timmy." She widened her smile. "You see, you and I are talking about how you feel. We're bringing it out—not keeping the pain locked up inside" She held him again and stared at the wall above his dresser.

Janet didn't really see the posters of the 'Doors' or 'Darth Vader.' She didn't notice the time on the clock radio, which shared the top of the dresser with a dusty collection of plastic, model cars and an eight-inch 'Wookie' doll with its right leg missing. If she had paid attention to the clock she might never have resolved the emotional upset of her son's traumatic morning. She would not have gained the release she was feeling from the trap of her own guilt.

"I still don't get it."

"The awful anger you saw between your dad and me had very little to do with the stupid things we fought about." She pulled away to see his face.

"I know." He wiped his nose again. "You and dad hollered about dumb stuff. My friends were fighting over a comment Johnny made about Carolyn's fancy car, an' about other junk—it didn't make any sense."

Janet kissed Timmy high on his forehead. "The words usually don't. The anger does because it comes from something deeper." She kissed him again and a tiny piece of ice seemed to poke into her heart. A chill crawled up over her chest and ran along her arms.

"You mean the crap about jobs and the car wasn't what they were yelling about?"

"Part of it maybe." She pulled her son close once more. "Oh, Timmy ...," she whispered and rocked the boy. "Someday it'll come together for you ... believe me, it really will."

"Why only part, Mom? How come?" He did feel better.

"Some people carry hurts for a long time. Guilt really. Then one day a lover or friend says something. Innocent mostly—and wham!" Janet pushed back. "All the ache and pain comes flooding out and the person hurting the most cuts the other to pieces." She pulled him to her one more time "The other—the one having no idea what they did wrong—reacts and chops back with sharper, fatal words that kill what they both really want." Janet threw her arms around Timmy and hugged him tight.

The ice she felt earlier pushed deeper into her heart and filled her eyes with bitter tears. "You're only twelve and your dad and I burned a hole in your life. It's wrong." Janet held her son tighter and kissed him on the head. Her fresh tears rolled off her delicate chin.

"Mom! I can't breathe."

"Sorry." Janet sat back, touched her son's face. She saw the clock. "I'm late!" She stood abruptly. "Hang on to all of this." She brushed the front of her robe. "Your friends have a good chance of getting things together because they're communicating early in the relationship, if they have one, there's hope. Take my word—they can make it." She looked at the clock again. "Are you okay?"

"Yeah ... I guess." He watched her fluff her hair.

"Good." She viewed the room with a critical eye. "Clean this place up. Then take a shower—you stink." She smiled.

"You smell nice, Mom." Timmy was closer to his mother that morning than he had been since the divorce.

"Thank you. A girl needs to hear that from a man." She looked at him for a moment and added, "Be here when Beth gets home—I'll see you after work."

"I will, Mom. Hey—I think you're special."

* * * *

Reach out from your storm.
Reach out to me. I'll hold your hand.

Bring me your frustrations, anger, tears
and your wrath.

I'll toss them into the night
and bring back a handful of stars.
I'll make you laugh.

Fight against your demons and thorns.
Fight hard in your time of trial.

Give me your hurts, aches and your pain.

I'll take them and give back a smile.

* * * *

Chapter Nine
Considering the Future

11:30 AM – THAT SAME DAY:

The university cafeteria was half full when John and Professor Lawrence enjoyed lunch. They were seated at a table near the center of the dining hall. The absence of students made the room seem larger and allowed conversation to echo off the yellow and white tile walls.

Professor Lawrence took a sip of coffee, and then placed the cup into its chipped saucer. He was a thoughtful man and John's forthcoming absence weighed on his mind. "While you're away, you should give serious consideration to the opportunity here."

"I intend to." John was still dealing with the abrasive encounter between him and Carolyn a few hours earlier. He wanted to see her again—he had to.

"Your work here may be a turning point in

your life. You've been very consistent. I think you're right for the job. I'd like to see you on staff."

John wiped his mouth with a paper napkin, looked down at the second half of his chicken salad sandwich.

Doctor Lawrence felt a sting of irritation at his assistant's lack of eye contact.

John shook a few extra grains of pepper into his vegetable beef soup, which steamed wonderful homemade aroma in front of him. He crunched a ruffled potato chip and continued to stare. The thought of working at the university full time churned through various compartments of his mind. Accepting the job, if he got it, meant facing a long-term responsibility. It also demanded accountability. That suppressed specific freedoms. Marriage carried the same order. He had failed in that institution and felt one-hundred percent accountable.

"You're right." he shifted his glance to Lawrence. "Anybody else would give their left nut to have the shot I got here, but I'm afraid of it." He crumpled his napkin and took a long drink from his carton of milk.

Dr. Lawrence regarded his student with serious question. "What are you telling me?" He shoved the spoon into *his* bowl. The sharp *clink* of metal against the thick industrial china sent several drops of broth onto the table and turned heads at opposite ends of the hall.

"I'm saying. I'm usually good for about six months at something. Then it goes to shit." He looked at Lawrence for a moment before shifting his eyes across the room. "My marriage turned to crap and all the garbage jobs since Vietnam ended the same way."

Professor Lawrence soaked up the spilled soup with his napkin and then looked at John. "You're not the only person in the world with problems." He spoke as he would to a student falling behind in grades. "You are however, the one I'm putting time and energy into because I believe in your ability."

John took a bite of his sandwich.

"It'll be a lot of wasted effort if you don't have enough faith in yourself to make it work." He studied the younger man. He hoped his statement would wrench an introspective response.

John stopped chewing, glanced toward the windows and drank from the milk carton. He smiled and looked into his friend's eyes. "Dealing with me has got to be a challenge."

"It is. Sometimes you're a pain in the ass, but I like you." He buttered a slice of bread. "I don't want to see you make costly mistakes."

"Thanks for caring. I do value your advice." He diverted his attention to a pair of co-eds who were carrying their trays toward a table behind Dr. Lawrence. An image of Carolyn flashed through his mind. He saw her in the memory of their first meeting as she brushed her hair back from her face and smiled *hello.* Then he remembered the anger in her dark eyes just a few hours ago. He shuddered. The mental picture broke up and fell away like a fully-assembled jigsaw puzzle suddenly scattered in all directions. "That's the way it's been. I've made several expensive screwups."

"So have I, but I've managed to learn from them."

"Yeah, I thought I had too." He shook his head. "Just when I think everything's together the bolts bust loose and the whole damn thing falls apart." He took his eyes off Lawrence and looked down.

"Cut the bullshit." Lawrence swallowed a bite of broth-soaked bread.

"What bullshit?" John looked startled. That kind of directness was rare from Professor Lawrence unless he was dealing with the track team.

"Yours, John." He leaned forward. A slight redness streaked his face. "You're beating yourself over the head with a club carved out of self-pity." The man's eyes narrowed in a spark of caring anger. "You give up." Lawrence cocked his head and took a quick breath. "Yes, you do." He wiped his chin with his napkin and *clinked* the spoon into the bowl again. "And that's the bullshit right there. We're friends, but occasionally you make me angry and this is one of those times." The professor spread his hands in a gesture of confusion and leaned back. "Dammit! You've got everything it takes to be successful in anything you choose." He shook his head. "Yet, here you sit—feeling sorry. Instead of taking hold of something solid, you back away trying to find an out. *The whole world's against me and I don't know why.* That's your lament John—and it's pure bullshit!" Lawrence turned his eyes toward the huge windows along the south wall of the dining hall and let out a slow breath.

John shifted in his chair and cleared his throat. The lecture brought an image of his father to mind. The old man always judged him in a harsh way and talked down to him. The scolding left a lasting scar. John looked across the dining hall. The memory flooded in.

* * * *

You get yourself a job working with your hands. Boy—that's how a man earns his keep.

* * * *

The haunting, rasping sound of his dead father's litany filled his head. Over and over—the same thing, in different words each time, but the same thing nevertheless.

* * * *

If your back ain't sore and your arms don't ache—you ain't doing right by the man. Plain and simple. A man's work is seen in the dirt under his nails and blisters on his hands. There ain't no other way. Not for the likes of us.

* * * *

The hollow sound of the words echoed off the walls of John's mind and rolled over him in a creeping shiver.

His father's statement was twelve years old, but there was an earthly truth to it. His father never got beyond labor, but had saved like a miser all his life. John couldn't deal with hard work for more than a week at a time. They were constantly at odds about it, right to his father's grave.

The echoes of that bitter-sad time continued. Lawrence had triggered them.

* * * *

What work ya got now, Boy?

* * * *

Another cutting memory sliced through John's heart. The wheezing, dying words drifted out of his father's sickness and slapped John as he stood beside the old man's hospital bed.

* * * *

S'pose now you'll feed off my insurance money and make it harder on your mother.

* * * *

The indictment hung in the air like a foul medicine smell. The dying man had gripped John's hand.

* * * *

I made investments, Boy, but you ain't earned any of them yet.

* * * *

The sting of his father's last comments dug a hole in John's heart. He had placed a single rose on the old man's casket at the graveside services. *A thorn pricked his finger as he did.*

John took an emergency leave from Vietnam to be with his father at the last. Their dislike for each other was buried with the old man under a headstone which proclaimed: *Saul L. Freeman: A man who loved his family and was a good father, may he rest in peace.*

He shook his head to throw off the vision—it didn't go away. He crushed the milk carton, dribbling the remaining contents onto his plate.

* * * *

The old man never saw things any other way—it was always his value.

* * * *

The memory found its way to his voice. "Never mine. He couldn't understand I wanted something more than a broken back." John looked up. Dr. Lawrence was staring at him. "I'm sorry ... I must've been thinking out loud." He turned away and put the milk carton down.

"Who didn't understand?" Lawrence looked at him with concern.

"I was just thinking about my dad." He caught the professor's searching look. "My father was in a rut and he thought everybody else should be. He never understood where I was in life or believed in what I wanted either."

Lawrence laced his fingers in front of him and regarded John seriously. "You think I don't understand? Is that what you meant?"

John thought a moment then answered without looking at the professor. "No, it's different with you—you do understand ... and I hear you clearly." He turned and met Lawrence's eyes. "You're right. I do try to find a way out. Sometimes I blame everything in the world but myself." He glanced down at the table. "I need the time away. I'll come back with the right answer, I promise." He looked up again and found it difficult to hold eye contact with the professor.

"I hope so. I'd like to see it work out for you, but the outcome is in your hands and you know that." He unclasped his fingers and started loading up his tray.

"I want to make the right decision this time—once and for all."

Lawrence slid his chair back and stopped. "Maybe you should get your mind off yourself and put it onto someone else." He smiled.

"Would you like to clarify that?"

"I was thinking in terms of a woman. Maybe a date or two." He stood and pushed his chair into the table.

"Dates? They're easy. It's relationships I have trouble with." Both men laughed and carried their trays toward the dining hall's south exit.

John's mind found Carolyn's image staring at him from the open window of her Mercedes. He had made a dumb comment about her car.

* * * *

I didn't connect you with the Benz.

* * * *

He waited while Dr. Lawrence cleared a space for their trays.

* * * *

Yes, ladies and gentlemen, me, John Freeman. The man who makes the worst comments at the worst time.

* * * *

The same chill crawled through him when Carolyn drove off in disgust.

* * * *

Beware the thorns.
They will draw blood.

Chapter Ten
A time to turn

Saturday morning found the entire San Diego coast covered with a thick blanket of fog. The damp, misty fingers reached into the city and shrouded the skyline.

John ran north along the surf when he saw her. The woman was more than attractive. He was drawn to her as he hadn't been drawn to any other woman since Christine.

She toweled off beside her car, the way she had the day before.

Carolyn draped the towel around her neck and looked up when he approached. An icy tingle walked across the back of her neck. She brushed her slender fingers through her hair setting it free to play in the wind. She grabbed the ends of the towel and looked at her sneakers.

Be careful, he's going to snap your head off.

He has to. Men need to get even. Watch him and keep your guard up.

"Hi." He stopped about ten feet from her. and removed his headband and wiped his face with it. "It's cold this morning." He said, testing her mood.

They both spoke at once.

"Listen, I didn't mean—"

"No, it's all right—"

They laughed together.

"Look, I'm not really that bitchy." Carolyn held John's eyes. Her mind raced through several apologetic comments. *Why should I give a damn anyway?* She patted both ends of the draped towel against her face just for something to do—something other than staring and looking stupid. *I've never gone out of my way to apologize before. What makes this case any different?* She sifted the thought through the screen she had installed in her mind a long time ago. *Have a few wires come loose? You don't say I'm sorry to any male animal. After all, they owe you.*

"And I don't usually make dumb comments like I did yesterday." He watched her uncomfortable smile soften and felt something warm happen. "I apologize."

"It's okay. Why don't we just forget Friday altogether and pick it up from here?" The thought felt out of place—dangerous.

Those words open doors, plant seeds—seeds that blossom into big trouble. Pick it up from here? Think lady.

Carolyn shuddered at the harshness of her inner judge and closed her mind to any further criticism. One of the protective doors she always kept shut had warped and sprung its latch. Something about John had gotten inside.

"Great. It's history." John stepped closer. He studied the look in Carolyn's eyes. He sensed some distress but couldn't hold on to it. "Have you seen Timmy?" He slipped his headband into place and looked at Carolyn from her sneakers up along her slender, shapely legs and well-toned thighs. He couldn't see her flat, firm middle. It was covered by a baggy sweat shirt. The fullness of her breasts wasn't lost. They pushed against the shirt and rose delightfully. She raked her fingers through her hair again. This time skillfully drawing it into a ponytail and attaching an elastic band. It was done in one smooth movement, an action that was inviting and sexy. John cleared his throat and glanced away.

"I haven't seen Timmy this morning." She slipped on her sunglasses. "He may still be upset about our little display."

"He's a pretty strong kid, he'll bounce back."

Carolyn tossed her towel into the Mercedes

through the open driver's window. "You know him better than I do." She turned away and opened the car door.

"Timmy helps his mom a lot. He's the man in the family since his dad split." He edged closer.

Carolyn slipped behind the wheel. "That's the real pain."

John closed the car door. "You're right. I'm divorced, but there were no kids, thank God. Kids get hurt the most." He collected his thoughts and then spoke in a lowered tone. "The boy's shared a lot with me. His hurt goes pretty deep. I think the reason we're so close is because his father took off." He leaned on the car door.

Silence.

"I'd like to see him again." Carolyn started the engine. "Maybe I can say something right. I owe him an apology."

"You can see him tomorrow if you want to." It was an invitation, a back-handed way of trying for an unofficial date.

"That's right." She remembered the game. It's Timmy's big chance to show off. *All your Sundays are taken.* "I don't think I can, but I'll try." She dropped the car in reverse and held the brake.

"I'll be there." He pushed back from the car. "The kid would be blown away if both of us made it." John could see the tension in Carolyn's expression.

"If I can, I will." She released the brake and the Benz started moving backward.

"Do you know how to get to the ball field?"

"I'll find out." She stopped the car and looked at John for a moment "Listen ... you're a nice guy." She blinked, turned away. I have a commitment. If there's a way, I'll be there. Let's leave it at that." She smiled, but it was guarded.

"Okay." John nodded and held her eyes. "Will I see you here again?"

He's reaching out to you girl. That's dangerous. "I don't know—we'll play it by ear." She smiled and checked the time.

"Okay ... we'll leave it open." He hesitated. There was a moat around Carolyn and he wanted to cross it. Any poorly chosen words or wrong moves would keep the bridge drawn up tight. "I really would like to run with you again." His words drifted between them like the aroma of fresh brewed coffee on a quiet, rainy Sunday.

"I'm not going to run tomorrow, but Monday for sure. I think I'll do it here." She smiled, holding steady eye contact. "Now, I have to go." The wind played with the part of her hair that hadn't gotten pulled into the makeshift ponytail.

"Great." He grinned and leaned forward.

"I'm looking forward to it. I'll come early and be right here when you pull in." He touched her hand. "I'm glad I found you today." He stepped back and looked at her.

A tiny sensation crept around Carolyn's heart and worked its way to the pit of her stomach. *I like him.* She released the brake. "I'm not really a bitch." She looked back at him and drove away.

"I know you're not." He waved. *She will be hard to know, never fully understood—always elusive.* The revelation excited him.

Carolyn looked in the rearview mirror and saw him still waving. She laughed and felt the warmth around her heart again. *I am affected by him. It's dumb. There's no room in my life for this kind of thing.* She drove into traffic and out of sight.

The sun broke through and pushed the fog out to sea.

John jogged south toward his beach house.

The thorns of the rose
are always present.
They are always sharp.
Thorns protect the flower.
Beware the thorns.
Embrace the beauty
of the rose.

Chapter Eleven
An Easy Promise

Some two dozen male students, in track uniforms, were performing calisthenics on the infield of the UCSD main track. John glanced at the papers on his clipboard and addressed Dr. Lawrence. "Scott and Iverson are off on their timing and they're both overweight." He looked into the second row of students and spotted one out of pace with the group. "Williams! Get it together—its cut-time and you're making it real easy." He turned to Lawrence. "Any word on my time off yet?" He shook his head. Williams did some kind of dance in an effort to get in step.

"I told the boss it was necessary and he bought it." Lawrence grabbed John's shoulder and squeezed hard. "If you can get these guys in shape by next Friday, you're free to go." He looked at him. "I'm counting on you to come back with a clear head, and I mean it."

"I won't let you down, Bob ... that's a promise."

"I want to believe you." The coach glanced away to witness the swaying, bobbing Williams. He handed John a red pencil. "Redline Williams. If he can't make it by Friday—cut him." He shook his head and checked his watch.

"That's enough. Give them a ten minute break." Lawrence turned back to John. "This semester will be my last as an assistant coach and I can't think of a better replacement than you. I need to know that you're going to give it a lot of thought while you're gone."

"You're leaving the university?"

"No, just coaching. I didn't want to say anything until I had a chance to discuss it with the director."

"There's no way I can replace you. I'd be lost."

"That's not true. You just have to realize it."

"I can't even imagine handling these dudes without you right behind me."

"You damn-well can. The only difference is, without me, you'll have to accept responsibility and that's exactly what you need to get your life together."

"I'm not sure I can get this team in shape by next Friday and you hit me with taking over your job—that's a lot!"

"Yeah, it is, but we think you're the one to do it."

"We?"

"The director and I have agreed on you. Go to Texas, have your month off. Don't let me down."

"I don't know what to say."

"Don't say anything. Give these guys their break."

"Take ten!" John's order was followed immediately. Williams' butt was the first to hit the grass. John drew a thick, red line under the lad's name on the roster.

Lawrence walked among the sweating team members as they reclined on the grass. As always, he gave them encouragement. He spoke positively to Williams, not forgetting the student's redline. He would reserve final judgment until Friday.

John listened and watched. *He's confident and sure. If I can be half the teacher he is, I'll be successful.* He put the clipboard under his arm and grabbed the Igloo water cooler. *Blow this opportunity and you might as well hang it all up.*

Dr Lawrence *hissed* a sharp breath through his teeth and grimaced.

John set the cooler down and went to him. "Are you okay?"

"Just another little chest pain."

"There's no *little* chest pain."

"It's okay. Too much hot sauce on the enchiladas last night."

"You sure?"

"I'm fine." He stepped back to the bleachers and sat down. He drew long breaths. "I'm okay. Go ahead and run the team, I'll check timing from here."

"You're sure you're all right?"

"Yes, John. Start the exercises."

Events of the future are often shown clearly in the light of the present.

Chapter Twelve
A Nasty Confrontation

JOHN'S BEACH HOUSE SATURDAY EVENING:

He took a bite from his steaming TV dinner while opening his mail. "Shit!" He tossed the official letter on the coffee table and called his ex-wife.

"Christine, what the hell are you doing?"

"Struggling to get by,"

"That's bullshit an' you know it."

"Your birthday is coming up, John. I happen to know the endowment from your father's estate could increase. That means more money for alimony."

John looked at the letter from Christine's attorney. "You're asking for a two-hundred-fifty increase. That's half of what I might get."

"Fifty-fifty, John, that's the deal."

"You know what Christy, darling, I'm going to use my extra five-hundred and hire a lawyer to counter yours."

"You can't do that."

"Sit back and watch. You bet your sweet ass I'll do it." He screamed inside. "Consider your letter moot!"

"You can't afford an attorney."

"I can now. You're not getting a single dime more than you are!" That's not a threat—it's a promise."

He hung up.

The *sting* of the conversation cut through him. "I loved that woman once."

He threw his unfinished TV dinner into the trash and looked around the living room. *This place is a mess. So am I.* John called his mother.

* * * *

"Hello."

"Hi, Ma."

"Dear God, a miracle. A call from my son. What's wrong?"

"Nothing. I have good news."

"I need to hear this. You're coming home?"

"I got the time off. I'll be leaving for Huntsville sometime next weekend."

"That's wonderful. I told you I had faith.

That's good, Johnny. I'll tell everybody right away."

"I'm so happy, Son."

"Try to keep it small, Ma. "I'm driving, so I'll keep in touch on the road, okay?"

"You be careful, Sonny."

"I will. Love you."

"You've made me so happy."

"I'm glad."

"I can't wait. See you soon, Sonny."

"Okay, Ma, bye."

Despite their differences, John felt a strong sense of security from his mother. It would be good to see her again.

In a mother's heart,
her children
will always need
her nurturing breast.

Chapter Thirteen
The Ballgame

MISSION BAY PARK:
1:30 PM SUNDAY – ROBBIN'S LITTLE LEAGUE FIELD:

John arrived late.

"Ball four!" The umpire's call rose above the shouts of the crowd. Timmy had walked the *Tigers'* batter. Tim was pitching for the *Strikers.* It was the bottom of the third and his team had three runs down.

John shouted, "Take 'em out, Timmy!"

The boy spotted his friend and beamed.

The next player was at bat and ready.

Timmy wound up and threw his pitch.

"Swung on and missed." The voice came from the announcer's booth.

"Strike one!"

"That's the way to go, Son!" Tim's mom yelled from the stands.

The boy on first started for second base. Timmy spun left and threw to first. The player started back and got tagged.

"Out!" yelled the announcer.

Shouts and applause came from the Strikers' fans.

"C'mon, boy!" John shouted and clapped his hands.

The batter was in position. He was a southpaw. Tim shifted his stance and tossed a fast one right over the plate.

"Strike two!"

"One more, Tim–take him out!" John's voice rose with the fans. He was standing at the fence to the right of the bleachers.

"You can do it, Tim!"

John turned around to see who was yelling behind him. "You made it."

"Late, but I'm here." Carolyn waved at Timmy. He wound up and let it fly.

"Strike three!"

The loudspeakers blared. "Two outs and one to go."

Carolyn cupped her hands and shouted through them. "Shut him down, Timmy!"

John added, "Go for it, son!"

They watched the boy nod at the catcher, wind up and pitch.

"Swung on and missed."

"Strike three–you're out!"

Music started and the *Strikers* came off the field.

Timmy ran up to the fence in front of his friends. He shouted over to his mother. "Hey, Mom–over here."

Mrs. Collins climbed down off the bleachers and joined Carolyn and John.

"I want you to meet my friends."

"Hi." Janet smiled. "You're the people Timmy runs with?"

"Yeah, Mom. This is Carolyn and Johnny."

"Well, you look like a really nice couple. Timmy told me about you two. I'm pleased to meet you."

Carolyn glanced at John and shook Janet's hand first. "It's nice to meet you."

John grinned. "Mrs. Collins, it's a pleasure." He shook her hand. Timmy has a great pitching arm." He looked at the boy. "Won't be long and you'll be up for MVP, son."

Carolyn said, "You're doing great so far today."

Timmy blushed. "Thank you for being here. It means a lot." He looked back at the field. "We're up, I'm third at bat, I gotta go."

John winked at the boy. "Hit one out of the park. We'll be watching."

"Thanks guys for coming." He ran toward the dugout.

* * * *

When the game ended, Carolyn and John said their goodbyes to Timmy and his mom and headed for the parking area.

Carolyn checked her watch. "I believe we made a difference for Timmy today."

"Absolutely. He didn't hit that homer, but he drove in three runs to win the game four to three. How long were you there before you found me?"

"Long enough to hear you running a one-man cheering section for the kid."

"I guess I did at that." He chuckled. "Did I tell you how great you look?"

"I don't think you have, but I appreciate the compliment." She stopped. "You aren't too shabby yourself."

"Thank you, lady." They met each other's eyes for a moment. "Where are you parked?"

"Near the picnic area."

"Me too. I'll walk you to your car."

"Such a gentleman."

They stopped walking. "Carolyn, I'm babbling about nothing here."

"I don't think a compliment is nothing."

"I'm serious."

"Serious is not on my agenda right now."

"Would you like to have dinner?"

"A girl has to eat."

"You're being flippant."

"Am I?"

"You are."

"There's a line, John, please don't cross it."

"I'm not talking about a lifetime commitment."

"I hope not." *Commitment,* she thought. *Nancy's a lifetime commitment.*

"Just a nice dinner before I go."

Several members of the *Tigers* ran by shouting about how they lost the game.

"You're going away?"

"I'm taking a month off to visit my mother in Texas for my birthday."

"A thirty-day party. They really do it big in the lone star state"

"I may not be coming back. I need the time to get my head together. I have to see if I really want to go full-time with the athletic department."

"When are you leaving?"

"I have to work the track team through trials until next Friday. I'll leave Saturday. He watched her expression for any sign of agreement. There wasn't any. "A dinner date Friday evening. We'll run together with Timmy during the week and we can talk about it."

"I'm not sure, John. I can't run in the morning next week. I have to be at work early to handle a new client."

They reached the parking lot and stopped by Carolyn's car. "What is it that you do?"

"I'm in advertising and there's a major TV campaign that I have to deal with. I'll be running in the evening." She unlocked the Mercedes. "I'm not really up for a dinner date, John."

"I'm not *proposing.* It would be a simple dinner, a bottle of good wine and I will feel flattered to share two hours with a beautiful, fantastic lady."

"John, you should be in sales." She opened her purse, took out a card, wrote a number on the back and handed it to him. "My office number is on the front. My home phone is on the back. If we don't connect on the beach, call me."

John took the card and read the front. "That's the biggest agency in San Diego."

"Yes, it is."

"Is this a yes?"

"Call it a maybe."

"Carolyn."

"Don't say anything more. I have to go."

A few boys from the *Strikers* climbed into a nearby red van. They did a few high-fives and yelled about how they had won the game.

Maybe I'll win my game. John walked to his car with a smile on his face. He thought of how he once loved Christine ....

If I were a man of magic, I could touch you and make all your dreams come true.

There would be bright, warm sun in all your days. Every night would be filled with stars I had put there just for you.

If I were a man of magic, I could cast a spell to keep you a princess for all the days yet to come.

A wave of my hand would bring forth beautiful flowers I'd give you one-by-one.

If only I were a man of magic, your every wish would be fulfilled.

Each moment would be a gift of wonder for all the moments there could ever be.

I am not a man of magic ... just a man alone.

All my gifts to you are things we cannot see.

For Christine
John Freeman
1975

Chapter Fourteen
Hope and Hurt

JOHN'S BEACH HOUSE – MONDAY 5:30 AM:

Early traces of daylight pushed through a curtain of gray mist along the San Diego coast.

John came out on the porch with a cup of steaming coffee.

"Hey, Johnny!"

"You're at it early." He took a sip of the hot brew.

"I couldn't wait to see you." Timmy stood by the front steps. "You and Carolyn at my game yesterday, man that was the best—the best ever."

"It was for me too, champ. You have no idea."

"Yeah, I do. You guys like each other and I'm glad."

"We'll see how that works out." He took

another drink of coffee.

"Let's go find Carolyn."

"She can't run mornings this week, Tim. We'll have to catch her in the evening."

"That's out for me. Mom's working late, I need to take care of my sister when she gets home from school. Mom doesn't get off work until about six-thirty."

"That's good, Tim. You're a responsible kid. I admire that." *I should have more of it myself.* "Hey, we got the morning, let's do it."

"You're great—I'll beat you to the jetty."

"Not if I can help it."

They took off along the surf scaring a group of sandpipers and sending a flock of seagulls into squawking flight.

* * * *

CAROLYN'S KITCHEN – 7:00 AM:

"Nancy, you're being a brat and you need to drop the attitude right now!" Carolyn jotted some notes into her leather day-planner.

"Mother, you promised we'd have a picnic yesterday and you didn't do it."

Carolyn zipped up her planner and stared at the child. "Something came up. You know that happens." *I've lied to her again.* "I had to take care of some business."

"Business—it's always *business.*"

"We'll go to the zoo next Saturday, all day. You can feed the animals to your heart's content." An ache worked it's way into Carolyn's heart. *How many more times can I disappoint my little girl?*

Nancy controlled her wheelchair up to the table. "I see an empty plate and a glass of orange juice. Where's my breakfast?"

"Aunt Clara will fix pancakes and eggs for you when she gets here."

"I could starve an' die—then you could have your *business* stuff and not have to worry about me."

"That's a cruel thing to say. I try to do my best for you."

"Oh sure ... when is the ramp and the gazebo gonna be finished. I want to feed the birds."

"I'm having it done special and that takes time, sweetheart."

Mrs. Clara Nelson came in through the kitchen door. "Do I hear complaining in here?"

"Mom wants me to starve to death so she can do *business.*"

"Well then, I guess I came just in time."

Nancy grinned.

Carolyn went around the table and kissed the child on the cheek. "I love you, brat."

"Love you too, Mom—promise breaker."

Clara took off her coat. "I'd better fix this little girl some breakfast before she faints away."

"I'm not a *little* girl." She hugged her mother. "Really, Mom. All day Saturday at the zoo?"

"Really. As soon as you're out of therapy, we head for the zoo."

"Promise?"

"You got it." Carolyn picked up her day-planner and purse. "I'll try not to be too late tonight." She brushed a lock of hair back from Nancy's forehead. "I love you."

* * * *

SOUTHBOUND INTERSTATE FIVE – 8:00 AM:

Bill Ferris lit a cigarette. "When we get to the agency, you stay cool. I don't want any of that bullshit you pulled on the movie set. I'm gonna have trouble getting back in there because of your big mouth."

"Hey, man, don't sweat it." Alan Tagart took a hit from his joint.

"That too, dude. When you finish it, don't do no more till after we meet with Ms. Parker. She can smell that shit an' you can kiss any chance of work goodbye."

Alan Tagart grinned. "What's this Parker bitch, a saint?" He remembered Carolyn and how they did it all together. *A saint she ain't.* He thought. *She's a devil in bed.*

"She's a good lady and gave me a lot of commercial work. She'll consider you on my say. Just try to be a gentleman."

Tagart coughed. "She's a good lady all right."

Ferris fought the morning traffic. "What?"

"Nothing. Just keep driving, dude." Alan finished his joint with a long draw and held it. *Carolyn Parker, here I come.*

* * * *

THE COACHE'S OFFICE – UCSD:

John sat at the conference table going over notes on his clipboard. He looked up to see Lawrence take a pill. "How'd it go over the weekend?"

The coach shook the small bottle. "These did the trick." He put the pills in his desk drawer. "I can't eat spicy food like I used to. It's just indigestion."

"You're sure about that?"

Dr. Lawrence pushed back from his desk

"I'm okay. I'll be with you for today's workouts, then you're on your own through Friday."

"I can handle it,"

"Yes, you can, I'm counting on it." The coach stood, coughed twice. "You go to Texas and put your head together. That's important for both of us."

The team captain knocked on the open door. "The guys are ready for laps."

John got up from the table. "Thanks, Paul, we're on the way." He picked up his clipboard. "Let's go run the hell out of 'em."

* * * *

BROOKS & ASSOCIATES – 10:30 AM – CAROLYN'S OFFICE:

Carolyn and Sandy were evaluating the script for the Martin shoot. Sandy took a bite of cheese Danish. "Are you sure Carlton Productions can handle this job?"

"I have faith in David's work. He'll know how to deal with Martin."

Carolyn's phone buzzed. "Yes?" She tapped the script with her pen. "Call David and set up a session." Sandy took her Danish, coffee, the script and left.

Carolyn responded to the receptionist. "Sorry, what is it?"

"There's a Mr. Ferris here to see you."

"Bill Ferris?"

"Yes. He doesn't have an appointment."

"Okay, I have a few minutes."

"He has a friend with him."

"I know Bill, send them in." She went to the window and looked out across the San Diego Harbor. *I love it here.*

Bill knocked.

"Come in."

"Ms. Parker. I'd like you to meet my friend, Alan Tagart."

A thousand hot needles shot through Carolyn. She turned to see the two men. "You brought that man here?"

"What?" Ferris looked from Carolyn to Tagart. "You know her?"

"Man, I know her, right down to how she moans during sex."

Bill turned red. "Ms. Parker, I had no idea." He glared at Alan. "You son-of-a-bitch!"

Tagart grinned. "Hey, babe, you look great."

There are memories
That will soothe and
warm an aching heart
There are those that can
Shatter the heart of
A guilt-felt past

Chapter Fifteen
Anger and Pain

Brooks & Associates – Carolyn's Office

PART TWO:

"Ms. Parker, I apologize. Alan didn't tell me he knew you." Bill glared at Tagart. "You're a jackass."

Alan smirked. "Who gives a shit, Ferris? I'm here."

Carolyn stood behind her desk shaking with anger. "You don't have to apologize for him; he's sorry enough all on his own."

"C'mon, babe—it's been eleven-years. I thought it would be good to see you again. I think you were pregnant. How'd that turn out?" He sat in one the chairs facing Carolyn's desk. "Have we got a kid?"

She looked at Bill. "You wasted a trip. I don't have anything right now. Give us a moment?"

Ferris shook his fist at Tagart. "You cost me twice, man. You can walk your dumb ass back to LA for all I care!"

Alan flipped him the bird. "Shove it, wimp."

Carolyn gestured toward the door. "Mr. Ferris."

Bill shook his head. "This was not my doing."

"Close the door on your way out." She took a deep breath and stepped around her desk. "I can think of a hundred things to call you, but I won't lower myself to your level."

Alan took a pack of Camels out of his jacket pocket. "Looks like you got a hot gig here, babe."

Carolyn smacked the pack of cigarettes out of his hand. "Get on your feet and walk out of here while you still can."

"Hey, I could never find you. I tried, but you were gone, babe." He pushed the chair back, grabbed up his cigarettes and shoved them in his pocket. "It's like, you vanished, man. I wanted to work things out between us."

"You're a *low-life,* Alan. Whatever there might have been you threw in the sewer. She leaned against her desk.

"Okay—we made some mistakes."

"We? You arrogant bastard! My mistake was you!"

"We had some great times, babe. I had to get away for a while. I never did you any harm." He looked around the plush office. "I guess you made out pretty well."

"Harm?" Carolyn went back behind her desk. "You're a user, Tagart. You sucked me into your warped world, screwed up my head, got me pregnant and split! I call that harm."

"Hey, babe—you were an adult. I never forced you into any shit."

Carolyn's eyes flared and the veins in her neck stood out. "I said I wouldn't, but I can't help label the garbage you are." She slammed her fist on the desk. "You're a bottom-feeder, Tagart. I spent thirty-days in the Los Colinas women's lockup because you ratted on Aaron for dealing."

Carolyn's phone buzzed.

"Yes?" She glared at Alan. "It's okay, just a few more minutes. Thanks."

"Whoa, big office, intercoms. Hey, babe, you got it made."

"Shut up, Alan and listen. You cost Aaron two-years hard-time and it was you dealing the dope."

"Hey, it was him or me, so I dropped a dime on him."

"You trashed a friend and abandoned me with a baby in my gut—your baby!" She shook and fought back tears. "Why have you come back into my life?"

"I was concerned about you, babe. When Ferris mentioned your name, I knew I'd finally found you."

"You haven't been concerned about anything but yourself since the day you were born." She strained to hold her tears.

"I wanted to find you an' see if I'm a dad." He grinned. "You know, be a family."

"Family? You're out of your mind! There is no family—there is no child. I had an abortion!" Carolyn stood. The tears rimming her eyes were burning. "I aborted you at the same time!" Her heart raced. "Get out!"

"If I find out you're lying, I'll have your lovely ass in court." Tagart got up and pushed the chair back.

"Get out now!"

"I'm going, but you'll hear from me again."

"No, wait. I'm not letting you take your handsome face and tight ass and just swagger out of here." She picked up the phone and pushed a button. "I want security in here now!"

She smiled. "You're getting *thrown* out like trash."

Tagart leaned on the back of the chair. "If there's a kid, I'll fight you."

"By the end of the day, I'll have a restraining order filed against you." Carolyn stared at him through red eyes. "There's pot in one of your pockets, I can smell it. One word to the security officers and they'll detain you for the cops. Your sweet ass will be in County lockup before noon."

"You're making a mistake, babe."

"The mistake, Tagart, is you."

Two security guards came into the office. "Ms. Parker?"

"Him—get him out of here and make sure he doesn't set foot in this building again." She hesitated. "He has a buddy in the lobby. Toss him out too."

Alan held up his hands. "Ferris didn't have anything to do with this."

"He knows you—that's good enough for me." She nodded at the officers. "Dump him on the street with this piece of garbage."

Sandy ran into the office. "Carolyn, are you all right?"

Carolyn's tears flooded from her eyes. "No, I'm not."

Sandy went around the desk and hugged

her friend. "What was all that?"

Tagart shouted from the hallway. "You blew it, babe."

A third security guard closed the office door.

Sandy brushed a strand of hair out of Carolyn's eyes. "Who is he?"

Carolyn pushed away. "A nightmare. He's Nancy's father."

"Oh, my dear God."

"He doesn't know about her. I told him I had an abortion."

The wages of sin
plant seeds of guilt.
The harvest of pain
will be abundant.

Chapter Sixteen
A Time for Change

JOHN'S BEACH HOUSE – 1:00 PM Friday:

Coach Lawrence was pleased with the way John had handled the track team and saved Williams from being cut. John brimmed with pride and studied Carolyn's business card for the fifth time. Mom first. He dialed his mother in Huntsville.

"Hello."

"Hi, Ma."

"Sonny, what a delight. You're coming, yes?"

"It's in the bag."

"What?"

"I'll be there."

"You're leaving now?"

"Late tonight or tomorrow morning." He looked at the open suitcase on the bed. "I may have a date this evening, I'm not sure."

"Sonny, you're going out with a woman?"

"I think that would be appropriate." He looked at Carolyn's card again. "I'm finishing my packing. I just wanted to let you know."

"You're going on a date?"

"Yeah, Ma, a date, maybe." An image of Carolyn came to mind. "I hope so."

"You couldn't take Christine out before you come home?"

"Don't go there. I talked to Christy the other day. We're working things out."

"So, you two are talking?"

"Yeah, in a way." He glanced at his watch. "I gotta go. I'll call you after I get on the road. It's a long drive."

"Well, you be careful."

"I will, promise."

"You're making me very happy, Sonny."

"I know. I'll call you."

"I love you, Son."

"Me too, Ma. Bye."

He hung up and studied Carolyn's card again. This is it, call her now. He dialed Carolyn's office.

"Good afternoon, Brooks and associates, how may I direct your call?"

"I'd like to speak with Carolyn Parker."

"Whom shall I say is calling, sir?"

"Tell her it's John Freeman."

"I'll ring. Please hold."

Carolyn came out of the conference room to answer the buzzer. "Yes?"

"I have a Mr. Freeman on the line. Will you take the call?"

"Yes, put him through." She sat at her desk. "Hi, John." She leaned back in her chair and swung around to face the large window.

"You said if we didn't connect on the beach, I should call." He paused. "We didn't , so I'm calling. I wanted to catch you before you left the office."

"The dinner date, right?" She watched a giant Navy destroyer cruise into the bay.

"Yeah, that's what I had in mind for tonight."

"I'm not sure, John." Flashes of Tagart ran through her head. She remembered the ballgame and giving John her card. "It's been a really bad week. Maybe we should do it another time."

"Carolyn, I'm leaving tomorrow. I may not see you again." He was reaching and he knew it. "Dinner, that's all I'm asking."

Carolyn thought of John with Timmy. She remembered the grin on John's face when Timmy's mother called them a nice couple. "Know what ... let's do it."

He took a breath. "That is just fantastic.

Are you sure?"

"As long as you don't get serious." Carolyn smiled and it felt good.

"I promise, not one serious word."

"Warning—I'm expensive." Her smile widened.

"I don't care! I'll order the best bottle of wine in the house and prime rib!"

"That's my kind of menu. I want some kind of flaming dessert. "She laughed. "Nothing cheap."

"You got it."

"Excellent. How's eight?"

"I'll be there." The phone shook in his hand. "Right on the minute."

"You know the La Jolla Shores area?"

"Yeah, some."

"I'm at 1152 Sea Court. It's a cull-de-sac off the main drive."

"I'll find it. Eight sharp." John's heart skipped a few beats. "Thank you, Carolyn."

"Where are you taking me?"

"The Harbor House, on the bay."

"Nice. Get us a window booth."

"It's a done deal."

"Pull up in front of the house. I'll be waiting outside." She hesitated. "That's a must."

"Not a problem, just as you say."

"Good. I'm looking forward to it." Her

smile was brighter than it had been in days.

"So am I."

"We'll have a nice dinner."

"We will."

"Gotta go, John. See you tonight."

"I'm flattered. Bye." He hung up, stared into space and shouted. "Holy shit!" He shook with delight, grabbed the ad he had saved and called the Harbor House.

Treasure the moments you have today. Tomorrow is mere illusion.

Chapter Seventeen
Temporary Risk

CAROLYN'S OFFICE CONTINUED:

Sandy had entered the office during the last part of the phone call from John. She sat at the conference table looking over papers in a folder. "I have the Douglas file. Steve wants to review it."

"He's late."

"Yes, but on the way." Sandy grinned and sat back in her chair.

Carolyn took a seat across from her. "What are you beaming about?"

"Nothing, I just think it's about time."

"Time for what?"

Sandy turned the folder around so Carolyn could view it. "It's time Douglas understood that a sixty-second TV spot runs one minute, not fifty-six seconds or fifty-eight, but a full minute."

"This isn't about the Douglas project. You're bursting with something else. What is it?"

"I heard the end of your call with a man named John."

Afternoon sun streamed through the large, tinted glass wall that looked out over the bay. The light danced in Carolyn's auburn hair when she shook her head.

Sandy pushed back from the polished conference table. "Is this John-person a potential client you intend to seduce into a long term contract?" She went to the service bar.

"If you weren't my best friend, I'd be angry with you." Carolyn looked at the Douglas file, but didn't really read it. "John is not going to be a client and I won't be seducing him on any level."

"Excuse me?" She took a cup down from the cupboard. "If I remember correctly, last Monday morning, after the Tagart incident, you were ready to kill any man who even looked at you."

"John isn't anything like Alan, not in the least."

Sandy opened a box of green tea. "I assumed so by the cordial tone of your conversation. You want some tea?"

"Yes, please." She looked out at the tall buildings reflecting the sun from their numerous windows. "I like John. We're going to dinner tonight."

"What?" Sandy dropped her spoon. "You need tea." She poured hot water into both cups. "I love it. You have a date."

"It's not a big deal." She sat back and enjoyed Sandy's excitement.

"I want to hear all about him." She handed a cup to Carolyn. "It's hot. C'mon, tell me the details."

"I met John on the beach. We've been running together for a while. There's a mutual friend, Timmy. He's a young boy who thinks John is super."

"Is he?" Sandy sipped some tea.

"I've been impressed with how he relates to Timmy. And he's been a perfect gentleman with me. We met through the boy, that's how it got started."

"You're sure John's not just trying to get in your pants?"

Carolyn squeezed out her tea bag and wrapped it in a napkin. "If I sensed any of that, there would not be a date." She drank from her cup. "We went to Timmy's baseball game last Sunday and I got a better feeling about him."

"Then you've already had a date."

"Not a date. I met him there because I knew the boy wanted me to see him play."

Sandy wrung out her tea bag and put it in her spoon. "I think it's great. Where's he taking you?"

"The Harbor House on the bay."

"That's expensive." She grinned. "What does John do?"

"He's in the athletic department at UCSD. He said he's an assistant coach of the track team."

"He's a jock. Watch out. Those guys think they own the world."

"I haven't gotten that impression."

"My friend, you like this man, I can sense it."

"Yeah, I do and it scares me." She looked out the window.

"Why?"

"At first, I tried to push him away. I was sarcastic and acted like a bitch. John didn't run." She took another sip of tea. "The truth is, I didn't really want him to go away."

Sandy took her cup back to the service bar and rinsed it. "This is all good news. We've been friends for a long time. I'm glad to see you ease up. What the hell—you deserve a break. Go for it. Take a chance."

Carolyn finished her tea and got up from

the table. “I have things in order. I don’t need any upsets. Besides, John’s leaving for Texas tomorrow and he may not be coming back.”

“I’d be willing to bet that’s the reason you accepted the date.”

“Actually, you’re right.” She rinsed her cup and put it in the dish rack. “John might not stay away and that bothers me. At the moment, he’s a temporary risk.”

“Carolyn, you can’t be shut off forever. There are men in the world who are sincere, warm and really nice.” Sandy laughed. “Although, there aren’t too many of those left.”

“I’m attracted to John and I can’t figure it out.” She shuddered. “The last thing I need is an involvement.”

Sandy took Carolyn’s hand in hers. “Does he know about Nancy?”

“He does not and he will not.”

“The boy, Timmy, might be good for her.”

“Sandy, you know my rules. There are no options.”

“It was just a thought.”

“A bad one. There’s no discussion.”

“Okay, we’ll leave it there.”

“Good, thank you.”

“Hello.” Steve Brooks walked into Carolyn’s office.

She stepped away from the service bar.

"We're in here discussing the Douglas file."

"Great, that's why I came by." He nodded at Sandy. "Did you speak to him this morning?"

"I did and he was supposed to be here right after lunch."

"It's long after." He handed Carolyn a document of several pages. "This is the court order restraining Alan Tagart from getting within a hundred yards of you. All you need to do is sign it." He gestured toward the service bar. "Any fresh coffee?"

"I'll start a new pot." Sandy dumped what was left over from the morning.

"Carolyn, it took our lawyers three days to get an address for Tagart. He's living in the Los Angeles area and that's where the restraining order has to be filed. You sign it and one of our attorneys will go up there and file it on Monday."

"I'm grateful, Steve, and I'm embarrassed to have our agency involved in the mess."

"That's not a problem." He looked at her for a moment. "You do understand that the court order is just a piece of paper. If he wants to get to you, he will."

"Is he going get this order?"

"He'll be served, but that's all it amounts to. Tagart won't be able to get in this building. My concern is your house and phone."

"He doesn't know where I live and my

phone is unlisted." Carolyn signed the necessary pages and handed the order back to Steve. "Thank you for doing this for me."

"Hey, you're family."

Chapter Eighteen
The Date

John pulled up in front of Carolyn's house at seven fifty-five and switched on the VW's interior light. He checked the address on his note. She sure has a great place to park the Mercedes. He clicked off the light and drew a deep breath. "You're way out of your element here." He climbed out of his beat up VW and started toward the front door.

Carolyn came out before he got there. She smiled. "Mr. Freeman, you're two minutes early."

"Actually, I drove by twenty minutes ago just to be sure I had the right place." *She's gorgeous.* He gestured toward his car. "Will you be warm enough?"

"Do you have a heater in that bug?"

"Yes, I do."

"Then I'll be fine." Carolyn had selected a medium-length, black cocktail dress, a simple gold necklace and earrings and red heels. She wore her hair down over a white shawl.

John hesitated. "Maybe we should take the Mercedes."

"No way! I haven't ridden in a Bug in years—I love it." She took John's arm. "Shall we?"

"Right this way, my lady."

* * * *

Nancy pushed the curtain back from the side of the French window just enough to see. "He's cute." She chuckled.

"Nancy, you know better than that." Mrs. Nelson came into the room. The child moved her chair away from the window. "My stars, girl. Your mother would have a fit."

"I don't care. He's still cute."

* * * *

John drove up onto the street and headed south toward the bay. "Timmy and I missed you this week."

Carolyn adjusted her shawl around the seatbelt. "I thought about him. That poor kid has gone through a lot."

"I'll tell you, he was so pleased that we made it to his game. It was like the highlight of his month. He talked about it every day."

She thought a moment. "The boy relates to you."

"It's because I've become a father figure, I guess."

"He's found a friend in you, and I admire the way you handle the obvious affection."

"You do?" Something warm moved through him. He smiled. "You really do?"

"Yes, and that's part of the reason I agreed to this date." She looked at him. "I think you're okay."

"Well, I'm flattered."

"You should be."

* * * *

THE HARBOR HOUSE 8:15 PM:

John and Carolyn were seated in a corner booth with a view of the bay. The waiter poured a small amount of a choice Merlot into John's glass.

Carolyn smiled. "John?"

"Oh, yeah."

Carolyn and the waiter grinned.

John picked up the glass and sniffed the wine. "Perfect, thank you."

The waiter poured the rich red into each glass. "Enjoy. Your server will be right with you."

He looked at Carolyn as if he just saw her for the first time. "You're lovely."

"Thank you. You're nervous."

"More than you can imagine." He held up his glass. "Here's to our very first jittery date."

Carolyn *clinked* her glass to his. She took a sip.

He scanned the menu. "We're having prime rib, right?"

Carolyn reached over and took the menu. "No, we're not." She smiled and her eyes sparkled.

"What's wrong?"

"Everything." Carolyn sipped more wine. "This place is not for us."

"I don't understand. What is it?"

"I've been here a hundred times with advertising playboys and phony executives. It's all show, just like they are."

"I'm sorry. I just thought it would be nice."

"It is, but it's not right tonight."

"I blew our date."

"No, you haven't. I got a better idea." She reached across the table and took his hands in hers. "Let's get out of here."

John dropped a twenty on the table and waved at a waiter. "That's for the wine. We're leaving."

* * * *

When they reached the foyer the head waiter approached. "Is there something wrong?"

Carolyn smiled. "Not at all. We're going on a picnic."

John looked at her. "A picnic?"

* * * *

Carolyn hesitated when John opened the VW passenger door. "Would you let me drive?"

"You want to drive?"

"Mr. Freeman, I haven't felt comfortable with a man since they invented sliced bread—I do with you."

"I don't know how to respond to that."

"Don't. The keys." She held out her hand. "Please." Her eyes filled with excitement that appeared to make her look younger.

He handed her the keys. "You're amazing."

"I'm glad you think so."

* * * *

She drove the bug along the Embarcadero, past Anthony's Fish Grotto and the Star of India. She down-shifted to second and hung a left onto Broadway. "This is great!" They headed into downtown San Diego. "There's a Vons market on fifth. We'll get some deli sandwiches, a bottle of a decent red, a pack of Solo cups and a lighter."

"A lighter?"

"We're going to the beach for a picnic—we need to have a fire. We'll get some potato chips too."

"Carolyn, what is all this?"

She glanced at him. "All what?" She swung a right onto fourth street.

"What happened to the distant guarded, Ms. Parker?"

"You did." She turned left onto fifth.

"Me? I caused you to break out of your shell? At Timmy's ballgame you told me there was a line and that I shouldn't cross it."

They parked in front of the market. "And you haven't. You've been a perfect gentleman. Most of the men I've had to deal with for the past eleven years have been wolves. I expressed that to you, sarcastically, and I apologize for that."

"You don't have to."

"No, but I want to." She studied John for a moment. "The way you are with Timmy, that's nice. Tonight, when you picked me up, you were so polite, so shy, I felt at ease right away and safe."

"I'm not like those other guys, Carolyn. I could never be. That's not who I am."

"That's exactly *why* we are together tonight and the reason I'm having a great time." She reached out and touched his face. "Let's go get our stuff and have a picnic at night."

John held her hand and took a breath. "I think you're special." He pressed it against his cheek and grinned. "Let's go to the beach."

Things you cannot see

The words I keep inside and do not say
tell of your magic, your mystery, and the
beauty of your smile. You cannot hear
them,
but they are there.

I have taken these things and some of the
elusiveness from your spirit.

I've put them in a tiny box. You cannot see
them but they are
there.

They are the treasures of the things you
cannot see.

Chapter Nineteen
The Picnic

Carolyn drove the VW south on Interstate Five and took the exit to the Coronado Bay Bridge. "I know a perfect spot near the Hotel Dell. "I haven't been over here in months."

John looked out at the San Diego skyline. "I was here early last summer with my ex."

"Girlfriend?"

"Wife."

She pulled the bug through the toll booth and drove toward Orange Avenue.

* * * *

A few minutes later they parked near a set of stairs leading to the beach. There was enough light coming from the hotel so they could see the way down the steps. John handed the bottle of wine to Carolyn. "You take this, I'll bring the food."

"Wait." She removed her heels. "I can't walk on the beach in these." She set them on the top step. "Okay, let's go."

"You're sure you want to do this?"

Carolyn studied John's shadowed face and smiled. "I'm sure."

The breeze off the ocean was easy, but it was chilly. John took off his sports coat and draped it over Carolyn's shoulders. "I don't want you to catch cold."

She held the bottle of wine and took his arm. "Help me down the stairs."

They made their way to a place near a fire ring and sat down. John took the sandwiches and the lighter out of the bag. "Here, hang on to these." He carried the lighter and the paper bag to the fire ring. "There's got to be some drift wood around here somewhere."

"You're a boy scout, John."

"I was once." He broke up some small pieces of driftwood and piled them onto the paper. "Just wait. We'll have a roaring fire in a minute."

"Roaring, I doubt."

John lit the bag and fanned the small flames. "It'll catch."

Carolyn laughed. "Come sit, we'll eat."

"Let me get some more wood. He walked off toward the ocean and came back with more fuel. "Now, I can keep it going."

Carolyn had opened the wine and poured some into two plastic cups. She handed one to John. "Here, take the chill off."

"Thanks. This is fun, I'm glad you thought of it." He watched the flames dance in her dark eyes. *Don't blow this.* He sipped some wine. "Hungry?"

"Yeah, let's eat."

He handed Carolyn one of the sandwiches and opened another for himself. He laughed.

"What?"

"I have to admit, I was a total jerk at the Harbor House."

"No, you were real, not a phony and I liked that."

"I was trying to impress you."

"You did ... in the right way."

"I appreciate you saying that."

Carolyn pushed her stocking feet into the sand. "There goes a good pair of thigh-highs."

John looked at Carolyn's long legs and a warm rush ran through him. *Easy, don't say anything out of place.* "The fire's going out, I'll get more wood." He dashed away into the dark.

Carolyn took a bite of her roast beef sandwich. Damn, I like him. It can't be.

He came back and dumped more driftwood on the fire. "That's better."

She poured more wine into their cups. “Sit down here and stop worrying about the fire.”

“Just wanted to keep you warm.”

“Your tweed jacked is doing that. You don’t wear tweed in the spring. Never mind, that’s more of what I like about you. You’re real, and I’m not ready to deal with that.”

“I don’t understand.”

“I was afraid something like this would happen.”

“Like what?”

“Enjoying this evening with you and having a great time.”

The wind picked up with the incoming tide and sent a sharp chill through him. “Wasn’t that the whole idea?”

“It was and I’m having trouble with it.”

“Carolyn, what in hell are you talking about?”

“I’m not really sure right now. It’s just me.” She looked north along the beach where other people had fires burning. “I’m confused. I’ve made a point of not thinking about having a good time, let alone enjoying the company of a man.”

He sat beside her and tossed another piece of wood into the fire. “If it means anything, I’ve shied away from the same things until I met

Ms. Carolyn Parker."

"What, the company of a man?" She laughed and pulled John's jacket tighter around her shoulders.

"Funny. You see, we're both having fun. What in hell can be wrong with that?"

"I don't know, maybe nothing, maybe a lot." She pushed her feet into the sand. "I have no answers. It could be the wine, the sea breeze. Even the freedom of this crazy date." She took a sip from her cup. "I'm all dressed for dinner and here we are, sitting on a beach eating deli sandwiches at nine fifteen on a Friday night."

"And I think it's great."

"So do I." She caught a breath. "That's the problem."

"Why is it a problem?"

"Have you been listening to what I've said?"

"Every word and you're not making any sense."

"No, it doesn't—I feel good being here with you and that wasn't supposed to happen."

He watched Carolyn's hair toss about her shoulders with a gust of sea breeze. Her eyes shined in the fading firelight. A warm rush crept through him. "I wanted that to happen." He threw a stick of driftwood out toward the ocean. "Dammit! Why does it have to be a problem?"

"I'm afraid of you." Carolyn dropped the rest of her sandwich into what was left of the fire.

"Excuse me?"

"Listen to me. I see you and I think of Sunday dinners, picnics and trimming a Christmas tree. I don't say these things. I haven't felt them in eleven years!" She finished her cup of wine. "That's the problem. I can't handle you in my life right now."

"Okay—I get the message!" He got up and scooped sand onto the remains of the fire. "I'm on my way in the morning. I may not have wanted to come back. You've made me think I might want to take the job at UCSD."

"I'm sorry. I didn't mean to spoil our picnic."

"Hey, it was your idea. We had fun."

"You're mad."

"No, not mad. Most of the time people aren't honest with one another. I'm glad you were able to say what you feel. I can't say I like hearing those words, but I can deal with it."

"I'm sorry, John." She stood and brushed the sand off the back of her dress.

"If I do decide to come back, may I call you?"

"I'll have to think about that." She looked at him for a moment. "No, I don't. If you decide to come back, I want you to call."

"Thank you."

"Would you help me up the stairs so I don't break my neck?"

He put his arm around her and walked her to the stairs. "Watch your step, use the railing."

Carolyn turned to him. "I'm glad we went out tonight. Forgive me for acting crazy and saying too much."

"Lady, I can forgive you for anything."

"It wasn't the wine." She kissed him. "I like you, Mr. Freeman."

* * * *

Occasionally the
stem of the rose
has no thorns
at all.

Chapter Twenty
Gentle Goodbye

John drove back from the beach. Most of the short trip was in silence. He parked the VW in front of Carolyn's house and opened the driver's door. "Here we are, my lady, safe and sound."

"Don't get out. It's okay." She smiled at him in the dim interior light. "I really had a good time tonight. Thank you."

"Me too. Your picnic idea was great." He closed the car door and they were left in the half-light from Carolyn's front porch. "I'll be gone by the time you get up tomorrow."

"I know." She adjusted her shawl. "What would stop you from coming back?"

"After this wonderful, crazy date with you, it would have to be something pretty damned important."

"And you'd be willing to forget the opportunity you have at the university?"

"If I hadn't met you I'd have no problem with that. Now, I'm not so sure."

Carolyn reached across the small interior of the VW. She pulled him to her and kissed him. "Go to Texas. Find what you're looking for. If you don't—come back. Yes, call me. Dammit, John—call me." She opened the door, got out, then leaned in. "The bottle." Tears flooded her eyes, but she wouldn't let them go.

"You don't need to be driving with an open container."

"Right." He took the half-full wine bottle off the back seat and handed it to her. "Carolyn...."

"Good night, John." She held up the bottle. "I'll save it." She closed the car door and stepped away.

John fired up the VW and whispered, "I don't think I'll be staying in Huntsville."

Carolyn waved and walked toward the house. She watched John drive off and went inside.

* * * *

Mrs. Nelson turned down the TV and got up from her chair. "Everything okay?"

"Yeah, I had some fun for once. Too much, I think." She set the bottle on the end table by the sofa.

"You like him?" She picked up the bottle. "I'll put this in the fridge." Clara hesitated. "Nancy saw him."

"What?" Carolyn threw her handbag on the sofa. "How did she see him?"

"I was in the kitchen and Nancy got to the front window and looked out."

"Clara, you know the rules. What the hell do I pay you for?" She took off her gold necklace and dropped it on the end table.

"I'm sorry. The child's just curious."

"You're supposed to be watching her!"

"Carolyn, I can't keep track of her every second."

"Obviously. That's how she got away from you, toppled her wheelchair in the sand and broke her arm. Not to mention getting a badly bruised leg."

"I'm sorry. Tonight, she just wanted to see you with your date." Clara took a deep breath. "She said he was cute."

Carolyn stiffened, walked into the kitchen and leaned against the counter.

"Come here."

"I'm sorry."

"No ... I'm the one who should be sorry."

She hugged the older woman. "Forgive *me.*"

Chapter Twenty One
Chuck's Bar & Grill

John came in through the side door, nodded at two guys playing pool and sat in a booth near the bar. He waved at the cocktail waitress and smiled.

Linda finished serving a couple seated near the dance floor and came right over. "Haven't seen you in a while."

"I don't have much reason to come here anymore." He loosened his tie and unbuttoned his collar. "I'll have a Miller's draft." He looked up at her. "I need a favor."

"I'll get the beer. You want popcorn?"

"Yeah, why not." The place wasn't busy for a Friday night. John remembered many nights there with Christine, Linda and her boyfriend of the moment.

Linda returned with the beer and popcorn.

"What's the favor?"

"Can you take a break?"

She caught the other waitress at the bar. "Terri, cover me for a few." She sat down across from John. "It's about Chris isn't it?"

"You still see each other?"

"She comes in once in a while, but we're not double-dating like we all used to."

"I'd like you to tell Chris I'll be gone for a few weeks. Actually, I might not come back." He sipped some beer and chewed popcorn.

"You're quitting the teaching job?"

"Maybe, maybe not."

"That's you, John. You don't know what the hell you're gonna do."

Two couples came in and someone fed the juke box. Kenny Rogers' *Lady* started playing.

"It's getting busy. I gotta get back to work."

"All you have to do is tell her. I'm leaving for Texas in the morning and I don't want a battle before I go."

"I think you'd better tell her yourself. She's been pissed about the late checks. " Linda got up. "Do your own dirty work. I'm not getting into this." She leaned on the table. "The beer's on me. Call Chris and face the music."

He got out of the booth, pulled out a ten

and handed it to Linda. "Keep the change. I don't want you telling Chris I came in here freeloading."

* * * *

"Why are you calling at this hour?"

"It's ten-thirty, that's not late."

"What is it, John?"

Two women came in right behind him. They were laughing and talking loud.

"Where are you?"

"I'm on the pay phone at Chuck's."

"What are you doing there?"

"It doesn't matter. I need to see you."

"Tonight? What the hell for?"

"I can't get into it on the phone."

"What are you up to?"

"I'm coming over. I'll be there in fifteen minutes." He hung up and took a long, deep breath. *God help me.*

* * * *

Carolyn finished a hot bath and wrapped her hair in a crisp, white towel. She put on a fluffy robe and slipped quietly into her daughter's room.

Nancy was asleep with the covers down

around her waist. Carolyn pulled them up to the child's shoulders. She looked at the ever-present wheelchair in the soft light coming from Nancy's small fish tank. A sharp sting struck her heart. She brushed the little girl's hair. "I love you, my angel. I love you with all that I am."

Nancy stirred and turned over. "Mom?"

"I'm sorry. I didn't mean to wake you."

"I saw John."

"You weren't supposed to." She brushed a strand of hair from her daughter's face. "How do you know his name?"

"I heard you and Aunt Clara talking."

"Eavesdropping isn't polite."

"Do you like him?" Nancy got up on one elbow. "I think he's cute."

"He's a nice man."

"But, do you like him?"

Carolyn kissed her on the forehead. "You're such a busybody."

"Do you like him, Mom?"

"Yes, I like him." She fluffed the child's pillow. "Now, you go back to sleep."

"Will I get to meet John?"

"I don't think so, sweetheart. He's going away to Texas to start a new life. I don't think he'll be coming back."

"For sure, he'll never come back?"

"Nothing's absolute. The only sure thing

is that we have each other."

"If John does come back, can I meet him?"

"I don't know right now. We'll have to wait and see."

"I hope he does ... he's really cute."

Carolyn took a soft breath. And thought, *He's a lot more than cute.* "Okay, little lady, you go back to sleep."

"I love you, Mom."

She pulled the covers up to Nancy's chin. "You're everything there is in this whole world."

Chapter Twenty Two
Christine's Wrath

John sat in the car staring at the three bedroom Spanish style house he was still paying for. She hadn't bother to turn on the porch light. He gripped the wheel and took two deep breaths, got out and went up the gray flagstone walk.

Christine stood at the screen door. "John?"

"No, it's Santa Clause bearing gifts."

"Always a wisecrack." She unlocked the door and let him in. "I made some coffee. You were at Chuck's. You've been drinking."

"I had half a beer."

"Yeah, I'll bet." She pointed to an armchair in front of the sofa. "Sit, I'll get the coffee."

"Cream and sugar please."

"You need it black."

"Can we be civil for a change?" He glanced around the room. "How much of the alimony went for the new living room set?"

"All of it. I added five hundred. I need more money, John."

"That's why your lawyer sent the letter?" He held his breath for a moment. "You want new furniture so you go after a piece of my raise?"

She came in from the kitchen and handed him the cup of coffee. "That's how it works. Your income goes up, my alimony increases right along with it."

"The alimony is for support, not a new couch!" He put his cup on the table beside the chair. "Well, Christine, I have a hot flash for you. My income might just be getting reduced. When that happens, the alimony goes right down with it." He took a swallow of coffee. "How's that fit in with your interior decorating scheme?"

"What are you talking about?"

"I'm leaving for Texas in the morning and I may not be coming back."

"You're leaving the university?"

"Quite possibly. I'm going home for my birthday and there are job offers there. That's the reason I wanted to see you tonight." He drank more coffee. "I'd hoped we could work something out until I know what I intend to do."

Christine sat back on the sofa and shook her head. "You're always a week or two behind. Now you're quitting your job?"

They both stood. Christine tightened the sash around her red silk dressing gown. "You're a loser, John—always have been."

"I didn't say I was quitting."

"Sounds like it to me." She went to the breakfast bar and poured more coffee. "You're running off to bum-screw, Texas, to get out of the extra alimony and hide your sorry ass."

"That's not it. I just need to get my head together."

"John, there are some things that can't be fixed. Your head is one of them." She poured two fingers of scotch into her coffee.

"Now who's drinking?"

"When I'm around you, I need a good stiff one." She sipped the brew. "I'm surprised you didn't wait to tell me about all this bullshit until after you were gone."

"I thought about doing that, but I felt it would be better to be up front with it. I came here to give you half now and I'll send the rest later." He pulled out his wallet.

"Half? I want it all, now! You are behind."

"Good god, Christine, your gift shop brings in a fortune. The alimony is pocket change." He took a check out of his wallet and glared at her.

"I don't care!" She swallowed another slug of spiked coffee. "You're obligated and you'll pay." She sneered at him. "Half payments don't cut it."

He dropped the check on the coffee table. "That's all you're getting right now. You'd better deposit it while I still have the funds." He picked up his cup and finished the coffee. "When I get to Texas, I might just close my account here and open a new one."

"That won't make any difference. You're still obligated." She sat on the bar stool and crossed her beautiful naked legs deliberately exposing them. Oddly enough she was wearing four-inch heels she knew excited him. "You're stuck with it until I remarry and that isn't going to happen anytime soon."

He looked away and drew a breath. "You know, Chris, there are three kinds of people in this world. There are good people, bad people and leeches. You, dear lady are the latter two." He adjusted his sports coat and stared at her. "I loved you once and I can't remember how that happened."

"That's all ancient history." She sipped from her cup. "I've heard it before."

"Just listen. I was in love with you. Everything about you was an excitement. Being near you, hearing your voice, smelling your perfume. Just touching you gave me a thrill. Making love to you was unbelievable. Where did all that go? How did all that turn to shit?"

"You're a loser, John. You were then, you are now."

"None of that meant anything to you?"

"It was fun for a while." She crossed her legs the other way. "You'll be hearing from my lawyer."

"Tell your attorney to stuff it where the sun don't shine!" He went to the door and turned back. "How could such a beautiful woman become such a witch?"

"Good night, John."

* * * *

FORTY FIVE MINUTES LATER – JOHN'S BEACH HOUSE:

He carried the third suitcase down the steps and pushed it into the front compartment of the VW. He slammed the hood. It didn't catch. "Damn." John shifted the luggage and closed the hood again. It caught. "Okay, now what's left?" He went back, cut the lights, locked up, and fixed a note and a check for the landlord on the front door. "That's it."

He climbed into the car, closed the door and shook his head. "What am I doing?" He thought of Carolyn and Timmy and looked at his faint reflection in the rearview mirror. Tears welled up. "Sonofabitch!"

John started the engine, backed out of the carport and headed for the freeway.

END PART ONE

Into each life rain shall fall

PART TWO

Chapter Twenty Three
You've been Served

LOS ANGELES, CA 2:00 PM:
THE ROYAL PALMS APARTMENTS AT THE POOL:

Alan stretched out on a lounge chair next to a tanned blonde. "Joyce, you look good enough to eat."

"In your dreams."

"I've had a few about you." He sipped a vodka-tonic.

"Alan Tagart?" A young man in a polo shirt and jeans walked toward the pool.

Alan turned. "Yeah?"

"Finally, I've been looking for you for two days." The young man approached.

"Who the hell are you?"

"Just a messenger." He held out an envelope.

Tagart took it automatically. "What's this?"

"You've been served. Have a nice day." Polo shirt waltzed away and out the gate.

Alan got to his feet. The return address on the envelope was for the San Diego County District Attorney's office. "Carolyn, you bitch!"

Joyce laughed. "They're catching up with you."

"Shut up." He grabbed his drink and headed toward the apartment.

* * * *

Bill Ferris answered on the fourth ring. "Hello."

"It's Alan. I just got hit with a court ordered injunction, man."

"Against who?"

"Me, man. It's from Carolyn Parker. I can't get within a hundred yards of her or her office." He slugged down more vodka. "I'm pissed, really pissed, man. I want to do something about it."

"Stay away from her, that's all you can do."

"No, man, I want to get at her."

"Leave it alone, Alan. Violate that order

and you'll be in contempt of court."

"Shit on that, man. She's got a kid, my kid, and I know it." He lit up a joint. "She lied to me, man an' I want payback."

"You're messin' with major shit. Why are you telling me all this?"

"We're friends, right?" he poured more vodka into his glass.

"I'm not sure about that. You caused me a lot of trouble with the extras union. Remember?"

"You got work." He drank more booze. "Give me a break, man."

"What can I do?"

"I need to find out about the kid. You still selling coffee and doughnuts at the court house?"

"Three days a week. Why?" Bill hesitated. "Okay, I know where you're going with this."

"Easy, man." Alan took a long drag on his dope. "Those investigator dudes buy your shit, right?"

"What are you suggesting?"

"Hit one of them up for a favor."

"That's out—no way."

"I want Carolyn's phone number and address. I'll pay to find out if she's hiding my kid, man."

"If she is, and you're the father, she can

sue you for back child support. Are you ready for that?"

"I'll find a way around it. I want to hurt her, man."

"Not with my help. You screwed me up with Carolyn's agency already. I could count on two or three jobs a month. You got us thrown out of the building. No. You're all on your own with this one."

"Thanks for nothing, man. I'll hire a snooper myself."

"Do that an' you'll be damn sorry you did." Ferris hung up.

Alan downed his drink and fixed another. "Fuck you, friend." He put a roach clip on the remains of his joint, picked up the court order and ripped it in half. "I'm gonna give you some shit, Carolyn Parker."

* * * *

CAROLYN'S OFFICE – SAN DIEGO – 3:30 PM:

Sandy closed the Douglas folder. "It's a done-deal. The ad campaign's in the bag and we start shooting locally next Monday morning at seven sharp."

Carolyn took a breath and sipped some cold tea. "I don't want cost overruns on this account. We have to keep Jim Douglas and his overzealous director under control. They always think they're doing a remake of Gone with the Wind."

"I'll be on the shoot every day."

"Sandy, you're the best. Have I told you how much I appreciate you?"

"Not today."

Carolyn's phone buzzed. "Yes?"

It was the front desk. "I have a Mr. Ferris on three."

"What does he want?"

"He says it's urgent."

"Ask him what is urgent."

Carolyn looked at Sandy. "It's Ferris. Remember the incident with him and Tagart?"

"You had them thrown out?"

"Yeah, both of them."

The receptionist came back. "He says it's about Tagart."

"Put him through."

"Ms. Parker, I'm sorry, but I need to talk to you."

"I'll have nothing for you ever again. What about Tagart?"

"Alan believes you have a child. He thinks it's his. He's going to hire an investigator to find out. I just wanted to let you know."

"You're sure?"

"Absolutely. He wanted me to help him and I won't do it."

"When did he do this?"

"He hasn't yet, but he will. Alan got your court order this afternoon and he said he wants to hurt you."

Carolyn gripped the phone. "Okay, thanks for the warning."

"I'm sorry, Ms. Parker, I didn't know what Alan was up to."

"Nobody does, Bill. Thank you for calling." She hung up and looked at Sandy. "Tagart's hiring an investigator to find Nancy."

"That sonofabitch!" She pulled Carolyn's phone across the desk and punched reception. "Get Steve in here ASAP!"

* * * *

Steve sat across from Carolyn at the conference table. "Do you think his threat is for real?"

She blotted her eyes and cleared her throat. "Knowing him, yes, he'll do what he says. I'm afraid."

He stood and addressed Sandy. "Get our security chief on the line in my office. He reached across the table and took Carolyn's hands in his. "You're okay. Nobody, I mean nobody is going to get to you or Nancy. Mr. Tagart is about to meet a couple of guys who will set him straight very quickly."

"He'll get a stronger court order?"

"Something along that line."

Chapter Twenty Four
Home Again

HUNTSVILLE, TEXAS – MONDAY – 9:30 AM:

John stood in front of the two story, wood frame house that he grew up in. Nothing changes so much as it stays the same. He went to the front door and rang the bell.

Sarah put down the scissors from the dress pattern she was cutting. She liked to work at the dining room table.

"I'm coming." She went to the front door and opened it. "Sonny—oh my. You're home."

"Hi, Ma."

"My Johnny." Tears welled up in the woman's eyes.

John opened the screen door, dragged in a suitcase and gave his mother a big hug. "Good to see you." He pulled back. "You look great ... it's been a while."

He set the suitcase inside the door and they walked into the lemon-yellow kitchen. "You worried me, Sonny. One call from Arizona with so many more miles to drive."

"I'm here." He looked around the room. "It doesn't change. Your kitchen is exactly as it was when I left."

"I should change it?"

"I'm just thinking out loud. Don't change anything. It's perfect as it is." He looked at the little woman for a moment. "Come here,"

"What?"

He took his mother in his arms again, kissed her on the cheek, "I'm glad to see you." Tears stung, but he held them.

"I'm so happy you came home, sonny." Sarah used her apron to dry her eyes. "Your room's all spick and span and I put new sheets on the bed."

"Thanks. Let me get the rest of my things out of the car."

"Sonny."

"What?"

"You're so thin."

"I work out. I run a lot."

"Well, we'll have to put some beef on those bones."

"Somehow, I think that's going to happen while I'm here." He grinned. "I love you." He hesitated. "I'll get my stuff."

"You're uncles are coming to the party."

"Great. I can't wait." He shuddered at the thought.

A few minutes later he carried his other two bags in and set them in the dining room. "My birthday isn't until tomorrow. When are you planning to have the party?"

"Tonight. I thought I told you."

"Actually, I don't remember you saying that."

"Is it a problem?" Sarah stood in the archway between the kitchen and the dining room. "Everybody's excited about seeing you."

"It's okay; I just thought I'd have more time to get settled in." He picked up one of his suitcases. "It'll be fine." John smiled. "I need to get a short run, then I want to go into town for a look around."

"You're not upset?"

"No, no, not at all." He held out his free arm. "Another hug?"

Sarah put both arms around him. "I'm glad you're home, sonny."

"Me too." He held her a moment and kissed her on top of the head. "It'll be nice."

* * * *

John ran in place for a minute and leaned against a tree. “It’s too damn hot to run here.” He thought about running along the beach in San Diego with Carolyn and Timmy. "What the hell am I doing in Huntsville?”

* * * *

Sarah sat at the dinning room table and pushed the foot pedal. She ran a seam along the hem of the dress she was working on. “That you, Sonny?” The Singer muffled the sound of the back door.

“I’m in the kitchen.” He grabbed a bottle of Coke from the fridge and opened it.

“Did you have a good exercise?”

“I didn’t hear what you said.”

Sarah finished the seam and took her foot off the pedal. “I wondered if you had a good workout, whatever you call it.” She snipped the thread and held up the dress.

John sat across from her at the table. “I can’t run in Texas. It’s ninety-five degrees out there.” He swallowed a gulp of soda.

“You’ll get used to it after you’re here a while.”

“I don’t think I’ll be around quite that long.” He took another swig of Coke.

"You haven't been home a full day and you're ready to leave." She folded the dress and put the cover on the sewing machine. "I understand. You miss Christine."

"I don't want to get into that with you, Ma. I'm here for my birthday. You wanted the party so let's do it."

Sarah wrapped the cord around the foot pedal. "I said it before, Johnny, and I'll say it again." She opened the lower cabinet on her massive oak hutch and put the sewing machine away. "There's always a chance to make amends. Christine is a lovely woman." She closed the cabinet with a bang and took the garment off the table. "You were married in a synagogue before God. You both said sacred vows." She caught a short breath. "That was all for nothing?"

John stood and finished his Coke. "Damn it, Ma, accept it! Chris and I are divorced—it's done." He pushed the chair against the table. "That woman will haunt me to the death. I do not miss her!"

Sarah's eyes welled up. "Let's not fight."

"Good, I agree. No more arguments."

"I'm happy you're home." She smiled. "Now, I have to get busy."

He nodded. "I didn't mean to be harsh with you. Let's make the best of our time."

She wiped her eyes. "People will be coming here about eight. Your Aunt Sophie and her daughter, Cheryl will be over this afternoon to help get things ready."

"How is the old bat?"

"Johnny, you should not say such a thing."

"Aunt Sophie was always a pain in the ass." He laughed.

"She means well and she's looking forward to seeing you again."

He ran his hands through his hair. "Cheryl is still here?"

"Not everybody ran off like you did. Some folks stay close to home."

"Yeah, I guess they're afraid to look over the hill."

"What's that mean?" She pushed her chair into the table and adjusted the lace cloth.

"Nothing." He went into the kitchen and put his Coke bottle on the counter.

"Say hi to Aunt Sophie and cousin Cheryl for me."

Sarah came in behind him. "Promise me you'll be civil at the party."

"I promise." He hugged her from behind. "You're a peach."

"I care about you."

He pulled off his sweatshirt. "I'm gonna get a shower and go into town for a while. I need to see what's changed."

"Don't expect much. Everything's pretty well the same as it was."

* * * *

ONE HOUR LATER – TOM'S DINER:

Two guys sat at the counter talking and eating a late breakfast. The booths along the front windows had changed. They were now red and white vinyl and looked new. Chrome jukebox selectors were still in place, but no music was playing. The lunch crowd, if any were expected, hadn't started arriving.

He sat in the first booth near the front door. The waitress spotted him and came over. "Hi." She handed him a menu. "Want something to drink?"

"I'd like a nice, cold glass of expensive champagne."

"Excuse me?"

"Hi, Susan." He looked up at the young woman.

"Oh my god!" She grinned from ear-to-ear. "John Freeman!"

"In the flesh."

"I can't believe this. Long, lost John. What are you doing in town?" Susan flustered and took out her order pad. "I'm knocked out."

"My mom insisted I come home for my birthday and here I am."

"All the way from Hollywood."

He picked up the menu. "San Diego. That's a hundred and twenty miles south of Tinsel Town." He tapped the menu. "Can I get some breakfast?"

"Yeah, sure. Damn, John Freeman. I'm numb."

"I'm starving." He noticed her tired, blue eyes. "How about a mess of scrambled eggs, steak rare and home fries?"

"Comin' up." She jotted the order on her pad. "I'm stoked." She reached out and touched his face. "I'll be right back."

He remembered Susan from what seemed to be a long time ago. Things were a lot different then.

She returned to the booth. "Ya all look so good." She hesitated. "What about you an' Christine?"

"That didn't work out. We're divorced now."

"I'm sorry."

"Don't be." He studied her for a moment. "You married?"

Susan's grin turned upside down. "No, I'm not." She looked into John's eyes for a moment. "Prospects are a bit slim in this burg."

"There must be a boyfriend."

"I've had a few, nothing important."

The bell sounded. The cook shouted. "You're up, Sue."

"That's your order. I'll be right back."

He watched her go to the service counter. *Do I dare ask her?* He played with the tabs on the jukebox selector. *Yes, I will.* He sat back while Susan put his steaming plate in front of him. "Hey, that looks great."

"How long are you staying?"

"I'm not sure." He shook some pepper and salt on his steak and eggs. "My mom thinks I'm home for good, but that's not going to happen." He cut a piece of meat and put it in his mouth. "Excellent. Tom still running this place?"

"He died two years ago. His sons own it now."

He took a forkful of scrambled eggs and made eye-contact with Susan. He chewed a moment. "You open tonight?"

"For what?"

"My birthday party."

"You're serious?"

"Just as serious as how much I'm enjoying this breakfast."

"John Freeman, you're kidding me."

"Not for a second. The party's at about eight. I'll pick you up at seven thirty." He wiped his mouth and sipped some coffee. "Where do you live?"

"I have a trailer in the Garden Estates Park. I'm in number thirty six. It's on El Paso Drive. You turn right in the second entrance. I'm in the third unit on the left."

"I'll find it."

"Why are you doing this?"

"Because we had something and I've always liked you." He took her hand. "My mother has invited a list of uncles, aunts and cousins and I need moral support."

"I don't know them."

"I don't really know them either. They'll love you."

The cook looked out from behind the service counter. "Sue, could you get back to work?"

"In a minute, Sam." She looked at John. "We had something. It could've lasted."

"Let's have some fun tonight, okay?"

"I promise you that for sure."

He enjoyed another bite of steak. Susan looked back at him from the service counter. She smiled.

John nodded. *Mother and the relatives will be very surprised.* He finished his breakfast and left Susan a ten-dollar tip.

Chapter Twenty Five
The Tail and the Party

LOS ANGELES – MONDAY – 6:00 PM:
ROYAL PALMS APARTMENTS:

The wrought iron security gate slid open and Alan Tagart drove his Black BMW out of the parking area and stopped at the street.

"That our guy?"

The amber light on the gatepost shined through the Beemer's windows. Tagart lit a smoke.

Nick Falon glanced at the photo on the Ford's dashboard. "He's the dude."

Ken Tracy started the Crown Vic. "Let's make this quick and painful then catch a great dinner downtown."

"No argument here."

Alan pulled out and turned right onto Lexington.

Ken switched on the Ford's lights and followed two cars behind. Nick looked at the picture. "This guy's a real lady killer."

"Apparently he picked the wrong woman this time."

Tagart turned left onto Sunset and merged into traffic. Ken did the same and stayed one car back. "He's going toward West Hollywood."

"Ya know, it used to be nice to come here." Nick adjusted the forty-five in his shoulder holster. "Now it's Shit City."

* * * *

Ten minutes later, Tagart drove into the parking lot alongside the Ventura Club.

Ken stopped in the fire lane out front. Flashing green neon pulsed through the Ford's windows. "Give him time to get inside."

"What a scum-hole." Nick watched two street hookers eyeing their car. "In another two minutes we're going to get solicited."

"I'll take it around back."

* * * *

HUNTSVILLE - SARAH'S HOUSE – 8:45 PM: JOHN'S BIRTHDAY PARTY:

Aunt Sophie whispered to John's mother. "Who's that with Johnny?"

"Susan—Susan Williams, I think. Didn't he introduce her to you?" She stirred the baked beans and spooned some into a chafing dish.

"Well, no. I don't know the girl. Who's her family?" Sophie glanced over at Susan and John. "If I'm not mistaken, that young lady has a sordid reputation here abouts."

"I have no idea who her family is and I don't know about any reputation." Sarah lifted the hot dish. "I just wish he'd brought Christine instead of a stranger." She carried the beans to the dining room table and set them down. "I wanted John and Chris to work things out, but he gets mad when I bring it up."

"Then they *are* divorced?"

"Yes, and it hurts my heart."

"There should be a law. A sacred, Jewish marriage gone to hell like that." Sophie caught a breath. "I'm sorry, sister. I just don't understand what the world's coming to."

"Nor do I."

Sophie covered a tray of warm biscuits. "They lose the good teaching of the faith as soon as they leave home."

"You be still. I don't want trouble tonight."

"In the eyes of God, they're still man and wife. Nobody can change that." Aunt Sophie glanced at Susan and whispered. "That girl is not for Johnny. Look at the way she's dressed. Her skirt's too short. Naked legs and arms and so much makeup. It's not appropriate."

"It's none of our business. Now let's get the rest of the food out of the kitchen." Sarah looked over the arrangement of hot and cold dishes. "Ask Cheryl to bring in the platter of deviled eggs. I'll get the roast."

"My husband has been staring at that hussy since John brought her in here."

"Sophie—the food."

* * * *

LOS ANGELES – 6:45 PM – PACIFIC TIME:
THE VENTURA CLUB:

Alan Tagart sat at the bar with his first vodka tonic and lit a Camel. He admired himself in the mirror just in time to see two men come up behind him.

Nick sat on the stool to Alan's right. "Not too busy tonight."

Ken took a seat on the left. "I'll bet this joint hops on the weekend." He grinned at Alan's reflection.

The bartender walked up to the trio. "What can I get you?"

Nick smiled. "Nothing." He flashed a badge. "We're having a private conversation."

The guy stepped back. "Got your ass in trouble again, Al?"

"I don't know these guys."

Ken nodded at the bartender. "We know *him.* Would you excuse us please?"

The man threw a towel over his left shoulder and walked away.

Tagart tried to get off his stool. "Who the fuck are you guys, man?"

Nick grabbed Alan's upper right arm. "Drink up, you'll need it."

Ken took the left arm. "We have a message from the PI you hired."

"What is it, man?"

"He doesn't work for you anymore."

"I paid him two-hundred-fifty in advance."

"Well, you're shit out of luck. We had a chat with him just before lunch. He quickly understood it was not in his best interest to keep you as a client."

Two couples came in through the front door, glanced at the three men and sat in a booth behind them.

Tagart took a sip of his drink. "You assholes are full of shit."

Nick opened his gray leather jacket. "You think we're playing games here?"

Alan saw the grip of the forty-five. "Hey, man. I just wanted information, that's it."

"Guess what, scumbag, we have a lot of it to give you." Ken patted the left side of his black windbreaker. "That thing you saw in my partner's jacket? I got one too."

Tagart stiffened and gulped down the rest of his vodka tonic. "What do you want?"

Both men helped Alan off the barstool. Nick whispered, "We're going out back for some fresh air and a nice, serious talk."

* * * *

HUNTSVILLE – 9:30 PM – TEXAS TIME:
THE PARTY – SARAH'S HOUSE:

John came back from the dining room with a plate of food and another glass of wine for Susan. She looked up at him. "Thank you, honey."

"My pleasure." He got more wine for himself. "You know, Uncle Sol, I appreciate your offer. I just don't see myself as a clerk in your hardware store."

"Not a clerk. You'd be an assistant manager. I'll put you in charge of any department you'd like."

"Department?" He sipped some wine. "You talk like you're running a Sears store. What would I be doing, arranging hammers and screwdrivers on a pegboard display?" He went back to the dining room and refilled his glass.

"It's a solid career. You'd be home and could take care of your mother."

"Pardon me, but Ma is well taken care of. Besides, we argue all the time." He looked at Sarah and smiled.

She didn't.

Uncle Mort, Sarah's oldest brother, spoke up. "You like cars?"

"Here it comes. You're gonna offer me a job in one of your dealerships."

"It's a good living, young man. What'd you have against that?"

"Not a thing. It's just not me. I couldn't sell a car if my life depended on it."

"What the hell can you do?" Bud Chambers got up from a nearby chair. He had married into the family. "These folks are offering you good jobs and you're shooting them all down." He went into the dining room and opened a cold beer. "You doing so great in California?"

"Better than I thought, I guess."

* * * *

Pattie, Bud's daughter, addressed Susan.

"Did John tell you about my experience in Hollywood?" She had long brown hair and a pretty face.

"No, I don't think he did."

Bud came back into the living room. "They don't need to hear it."

Susan sipped some wine. "Please, tell me."

"It was wonderful. I took acting classes and had to learn how to speak clearly and project my voice. I learned how to carry myself with grace and move in front of the camera."

Bud cut in. "She moved all right. Right through about seven-thousand dollars and straight back here with nothing to show for it." He sucked a gulp of beer.

Susan bit into a cold shrimp. "That must've been a good time for you."

"It didn't work out, but I loved it."

* * * *

Sarah got off the couch. "It's time for cake and ice cream."

John kissed Susan on top of the head. "I'm up for that."

Aunt Sophie made a face and went for the cake.

Susan reached up, pulled John down to her and kissed him. "Happy birthday."

He whispered in her ear. "It's not over yet."

She kissed him again. "No, it isn't."

The toast will always
fall
buttered side
down

Chapter Twenty Six
A Learning Experience

WEST HOLLYWOOD – 7:30 PM – PACIFIC TIME: THE ALLEY BEHIND THE VENTURA CLUB:

Tagart grinned at the two men. You guys are pissing me off, man."

"Turn around, face the wall." Nick Fallon waited.

"Fuck you both."

Ken Tracy stepped closer. "Here we are, trying to be nice and you come off like a stiff prick." He looked at his partner. "Can you believe this guy?"

"He's a real bad dude." Nick spun Tagart face first into the cold bricks. "Put your hands high and spread your legs." He kicked Alan's feet farther apart and patted him down.

"Hey, man, I ain't done shit." Needles of pain stung his left cheekbone. "I scraped my face, man."

"Good. Enjoy it." Nick stepped back. "Look what I found." He held up three dime packets of white powder and handed them to Ken. "Little coke for the nose Al?"

"You planted it, man." Tagart tried to push away from the wall.

Ken put cold steel against the back of Alan's neck. "Stand fast, asshole."

"My face is bleeding."

"That's nice. Try moving again and your face will be part of the wall."

A young couple came out of the side door. Nick held up his badge. "Police business. Have a nice night." The two people departed quickly. Nick waited a moment. "I got more treasure," He waved a baggie of grass. "It's at least two ounces and there are four rolled joints in the bag. We hit pay dirt with this one."

"It ain't mine man."

Ken put his gun away. "Turn your sorry ass around and stay against the bricks."

"You guys are cops?"

Nick put the goods in his jacket pocket. "We're the PCP Squad."

"What the fuck is that?"

Ken got in Tagart's face. "Protect Carolyn Parker." He stepped back. "We're the last two guys on earth you want to fuck with."

"I got the court order, man. I can read."

Nick moved closer. "You're a bottom-feeder, Tagart. You're sewer water, a drug dealer. We eat guys like you for breakfast."

Alan shook his finger at Ken. "You guys aren't real cops so go fuck yourself."

Nick's right hand shot up like a spring-loaded bear trap. He grabbed Tagart's index finger, grinned and snapped it. "Didn't your mother ever tell you it's impolite to point?"

Alan's scream echoed through the alley. "You broke my finger, man!" He slid down the wall and sat in the filth. "You sonofabitch!"

Ken hunkered down in front of him. "You have seven more fingers and two thumbs. My partner here would be pleased to crack those for you."

"No, please, man." He held his right hand in his left.

Nick grabbed Tagart by the front of his jacket. "Get up, you piece of shit." He slammed him against the wall. "We said we had a lot of information for you." He pulled a tight leather glove onto his right hand.

"No, please, man. I understand."

"Do you really?" Nick stepped back swung and bashed the left side of Tagart's face. His head struck the bricks with a sickening thud. Blood flew out of Alan's mouth. "I believe the message is getting clearer."

"I'm sorry, man." He started sliding back down the wall.

Nick propped him up. "Yes, you are one sorry bastard. I like to keep things even, Al." He backhanded him across the right side of his face. More blood splattered and he let Tagart slump to the ground.

Ken bent down and held Tagart's face up. "Do you know Carolyn Parker?"

Tagart spit blood. "Yeah, I know her."

"That's not the right answer." He looked at his partner.

"Nick, Mr. Tagart hasn't gotten the message. I guess I didn't make myself clear." He backhanded Alan across the mouth. The blood spray hit the wall and the left side of his coat.

"No—I don't know her!"

Ken squeezed Tagart's fractured jaw. "I believe he got the message this time."

Alan stumbled through his words bleeding from the nose and mouth. "I don't know who she is, man." He wrenched and tried to get up.

Nick pushed him back down. "What about the Brooks Agency in San Diego?"

"Nothing, man, I never heard of it."

"Bingo. That's the right answer, dude, you're doing well." He hit him again. "One for good measure, just so you don't forget."

A man came in from the parking lot and stopped in the alley. Ken looked at him. "Private conversation. Go on inside and have a good time."

The man quickly did so.

Nick stood and looked down at Tagart. "One more thing."

"No ... please, I've had enough."

"Listen carefully, you bucket of swill. We have a line on you, where you live and what you do for a living. Slip once and you'll have more than a broken finger and jaw. Are we clear here?"

"Yes, sir. I got the message."

"That's just fine, Al."

Ken bent down in front of Tagart. "I have a question for you."

"Don't hit me again, please."

"No way. Our job's done. I just wondered if you know of a good place to get a great steak and a Caesar salad anywhere near here."

"No, man, I don't."

"Not a problem. You have a good night."

"Yeah, I sure will."

"One other thing." Ken took the little packets of coke out of his jacket pocket. "This is not good." He opened them and scattered the drug into the wind. "That takes care of that."

"You bastard."

Nick held up the Baggie of grass. "Over here, Tagart, watch." He opened the plastic bag, took out the rolled joints and tore them up. He dumped the two ounces of dope into the gutter. "You need another message?" He went back toward Tagart.

"No—just go away."

Chapter Twenty Seven
The Party's Over

HUNTSVILLE, TEXAS – 10:00 PM:
SUSAN'S TRAILER:

"Happy birthday, dear Johnny. Happy birthday to you." She stumbled climbing the four stairs to her trailer. "Oops." Susan grabbed for the railing and missed.

"Easy." He caught her. "You've had too much wine."

"An' you ain't had enough." She giggled while trying to unlock the front door.

"Let me do it." He took the keys.

"I hope you will." She leaned against him and pointed to a silver key. "That's it right there, the big one. Just go ahead and push that sucker in."

"You could use some coffee."

* * * *

The blow dryer stopped. A minute later Susan appeared in the small living room. John poured her another cup of black coffee. "Feel better?"

"A little steadier." She tightened her powder blue robe. "Thanks."

"For what?" He put cream and sugar in his cup.

"For the date. For making the damn coffee and for just being nice." She sat on the couch and brushed her hair, which looked brighter in the soft glow of the floor lamp.

"It isn't too difficult to treat a lovely lady with warm attention." He noticed Susan had put on fresh makeup. "You look great." He got away from the table and sat in an armchair across from her. "You have a nice place here. I like the way you've decorated it."

She sipped some coffee. "It's a dump—a box with indoor plumbing. It's cold in the winter and sweltering in the summer. I can't afford anything better. I'm stuck here." She took a breath. "Trapped is more like it."

"If you're unhappy, sell the place. Pack up and leave."

"Where would I go? San Diego? What would I do there, work in another hash house?" She went into the kitchen, opened a cupboard and came back with a bottle of Jack Daniels. "Would you be at UCSD without the help from your father's estate?"

"I doubt it." He watched her pour the booze. "Is that a good idea right now?"

"It's the best idea at the moment." She downed a swallow of the whiskey. "I don't have a damn endowment. I don't have skills, John."

"You're young, attractive and smart. Find something you like and go for it."

"Sure. I could learn to cook the eggs and grits instead of serving them."

"You're being hard on yourself. There are opportunities." He felt sorry for her and he knew that wasn't needed. "What brought all this on?"

"Your party, that's what." Another sip of JD. "I listened to your uncles and how they wanted to bring you back here and suck you into their mundane bullshit. They're jealous of you. It's obvious. Then, that sad story from your cousin Pattie. The poor girl tried and didn't make it. They'll never let her forget it." She took another drink.

"No, they never will." He went to the counter and filled his coffee cup. "They love to use Pattie to justify themselves." He spooned in sugar and cream. "That shouldn't stifle you."

"You know what, John? I'll get up in the morning, take a shower, put on my uniform, make up my face and drive to the diner." She shook her head. "I'll serve breakfast to the same old men. They look right through me. They don't see me. I'll get a two dollar tip and a pat on the ass like I'm a pole dancer at a downtown strip club."

"I'm sure that's not what they mean."

"Trust me. That's the way it is." She emptied her cup and sat back. "Every day I hope some handsome trucker will come in, sweep me off my feet and take me the hell out of here."

"My birthday party stirred all this up?"

"You did, John—you did."

"I don't quite follow."

"When I recognized you in the diner this morning, I thought a blazing star fell out of the heavens and flew in the front door."

He laughed. "I've never been compared to a star."

"Is it funny? Maybe stupid?" She didn't smile.

"No, I'm sorry." Fever crept up from his neck and turned his ears red.

"You're sorry?" She poured more liquor and held up her cup. "Here's to a fantasy. A few seconds of revelation. A flash of the past. John,

It made my heart race. All of that going on in my dumb head and it makes you laugh." She drank more booze and stood.

"I apologize." His embarrassment glowed on his face like a red mask.

"Everything came back, John." Tears welled up and flooded over. "We had something, Mr. Freeman. It was damned great!" She opened her robe. "I even felt a tingle of hope."

"Susan—don't do this."

"I'm still good, John. Come an' get it." She fell back on the sofa and sobbed.

He went to her and sat down. "It's okay, Suzie." He pulled her robe closed and tied the sash. "You'll catch cold." He put his arms around her and brushed her hair back from her face.

"You used to call me Suzie all the time." She rested her head against him.

"Yeah and you called me Sonny an' ran away laughing." He kissed her on top of the head. "Are you all right?"

"I'm slobbering all over your shirt." Susan looked up.

John picked up a napkin off the coffee table and wiped her eyes. "You look great with red eyes."

She pinched his nose and grinned. "Always a wise guy."

They looked at each other for a moment. John kissed her on the forehead and gently pushed back another lock of hair from her face. "I think we should get you in bed. All that Jack Daniels will be knocking on your skull in the morning." He inhaled a breath of Susan's scent and the image of a long lost memory snuck out from the back of his mind. "I'll tuck you in."

Susan hesitated. "Where did it all go?"

"I often wonder about that, Suzie." He carried her to the cramped bedroom and helped her get under the covers. "You gonna sleep okay?"

"I'll be fine now."

"I'm sorry I upset you."

"You didn't. I upset myself."

He kissed her on the lips with the softness of a mourning dove's feather. "I'll come by the diner."

"No ... please don't, okay?"

He touched her face. "I understand. Good night."

Chapter Twenty Eight
Goodbye Huntsville

SARAH'S KITCHEN – MONDAY – 10:30 AM:

"Your breakfast is ready." Sarah set a plate of scrambled eggs, bacon and fried potatoes on the table. She shook her head.

John came into the kitchen from the dining room and put a third suitcase near the back door. "Smells great."

"This is a kosher home, Sonny, I'm being sinful fixing bacon. I should be ashamed."

He sat at the table and sipped some orange juice. "You're not eating it, I am." He picked up a piece and bit it in half. "It's good, you should try some."

"Don't be disrespectful." She sat across from him and drank light tea. "Your father would never allow that meat in this house."

"Dear old dad isn't here is he?" John munched the second half of the bacon strip. "Are we going to argue about food now?" He stirred his coffee. "You got started on Susan ten minutes ago."

"I didn't say she wasn't a nice girl. I said she's a stranger to us."

He swallowed some eggs and took a sip of coffee. "She's not a girl, Ma. It's the seventies. You don't call a female over eighteen a girl. It's politically incorrect."

"What?"

"Nothing. Christine was a stranger once."

"Yes, but we knew her family."

"OH for Christ's sake. Get off of it."

"We're fighting again."

"Yeah, we are." He ate another piece of bacon. "That's one more reason I can't stay here."

"You're always angry, and it hurts me, Sonny."

"I'm sorry." He finished his eggs and coffee. "You're right. Its frustration, I guess, but after last night I think I've learned why." He sat back and watched his mother take his plate to the sink and rinse the remains of bacon and eggs into the disposal.

"You were rude to your uncles, Johnny. They mean well."

"I spoke my mind. If that's rude, so be it." He got up from the table. "Actually, I owe them a thank you. They made it clear that I have a real future out in California. Not in Huntsville."

Sarah wiped her hands on a dishtowel. "You've been home a few days. You drove all those miles to just turn around and go back?"

"I came for my birthday, just like you wanted. The party's over, Ma. I have to get on with my life—my life. It's time."

"So, I should be happy about this?"

"Yes, you should." A door in his mind opened and let a faded memory seep in. *Sonny, your father has passed on. He's with God now. He always loved you. Papa wanted you to be strong and find your own way.* He took a breath and swallowed hard. "I have to load the car. C'mon outside."

* * * *

John slammed the luggage compartment of his VW. "All set and ready to go."

Sarah stood in the driveway and handed him a brown paper sack. She had tears in her eyes. "I made you three tuna sandwiches and put in some baklava for dessert."

He took the bag and hugged her. "I had a nice birthday."

"You stayed a weekend. I might see you next year?"

"Let's look forward to that." His throat tightened. "I love you, Ma. You're an angel."

"I would hope to be." She couldn't hold back the tears. "You always have a home here no matter what."

"I know, and it means a lot." He hugged her again. "Over the last forty-eight hours, I've come to realize what I'm doing at the university is just what I want to do. It's the best thing I've got going and I'm going to make it work."

Sarah kissed her son on the cheek. "If you believe it, it will be."

"I do, Ma." He held up the paper sack. "Thanks. I'll call you every time I stop for gas."

* * * *

Ten minutes later, John pulled up in front of Susan's trailer. He left the car running, went up the steps and taped an envelope to the front door. He whispered, "I hope this means something to you."

* * * *

At 5:30 PM Susan sat on the couch and read John's note:

Dear, Susan: I'll always remember the sunshine in your eyes and your sassy smile. I've named a star for you and called it Suzie. One day soon it will fall from the heavens and take rest in your heart. At that moment, all your dreams will come true.

Dream your dreams, they are yours alone. I'll always remember you.

Sonny

Susan folded the note. She poured a double shot of Jack Daniels. "Thanks, John." She lifted her glass. "Here's to my star."

* * * *

Another night ended in Huntsville, Texas.

Chapter Twenty Nine
Consultation

SAN DIEGO – MONDAY – 8:30 AM:
EXAMINATION ROOM FOUR – DR. BAILEY'S CLINIC:

"That's the bone in your arm." Dr. Bailey pointed to the X-ray of Nancy's break.

"Am I fixed?" She looked at the doctor and then her mother.

Dr. Bailey smiled. "You're good to go, little girl."

Carolyn let out a sigh. "Thanks to Dr. Stone, you mended."

Nancy held up her arm. "What about this?"

The doctor grinned at the child. "That cast comes off today."

"Great! Can I keep it?"

Bailey laughed. “Well, from what I know about fine art, that cast is priceless.”

“Mom, can I?” Her eyes glistened with excitement.

“It’s yours, sweetheart. We’ll display it on a shelf in your room.” Carolyn’s voice cracked. “You’re an angel.”

“Thanks, Mom.” She pushed herself forward on the examination table. “Will you sign it for me, Dr. Bailey?”

“I’d be most honored.” He took a pen from his smock.

“No, with this one.” Nancy pulled a thick blue Magic Marker from the pocket of her pink dress. “I want your name to be really big.”

“I’m flattered, but Dr. Stone did your surgery.”

“He’s a nice man and I like him, but I’ve known you longer.”

“Okay, it’s a pleasure, my lady.”

Carolyn looked away and tried to swallow the tightness in her throat.

A young nurse came in. “Are we ready?”

Nancy beamed. “Hi, Alice.” She held up her arm again. “They’re cutting it off today.”

“Oh, my. The whole arm?”

“No, silly. The cast.”

“Thank God for small favors.” She helped the child into the wheelchair. “Let’s get to therapy first, then we'll chop off that arm." Alice smiled at Carolyn.

Nancy shook her head. "Therapy. Phooey—damn."

"Nancy!"

"Okay, Mom."

Dr. Bailey laughed. "Bring her to my office when she's done."

Alice pushed the wheelchair to the door. "Right after we slice off her arm."

"Done?" Nancy leaned out of the chair. "Like a turkey on Thanksgiving. I'll be all basted, brown an' ready for the carving." The door closed behind them.

Carolyn walked to the examination table and leaned on it. "That little girl is everything in this world, Charles. You know that."

"She's a fighter and has more spirit than ten kids in her condition." He took a large envelope off the counter. "I want you to see this."

"Is it good?" She shivered.

"It's great." He slipped two different X-rays out of the envelope and put them up on the light-board. "I wanted to go over this with you privately."

Carolyn recognized the images. "It's the shunt. I don't see any difference."

"There isn't any change and that's the

good thing." He pointed to the picture on the left. "That was a month ago." He tapped his finger on the second image. "This is the shot we took this morning. The shunt is stable. Fluid is draining perfectly."

"She's improving?" Carolyn studied the doctor's eyes.

"Nancy is stable. Her brain activity isn't being compromised." He took the pictures off the light board.

"She's getting better?"

"Carolyn, you know the answer to that. Nancy doesn't get better. Don't think that can happen. I've never led you to believe otherwise. Right now, there is no cure for spina bifida. She's just eleven and doing great." The doctor switched off the light and took down the pictures. "In a few years maybe something will come up."

"In a few years my baby could die."

"I've just given you good news. That's the best we can expect for now."

"I understand." She folded her arms and stepped away from the table. "That precious little child is a cripple because of me." Carolyn fought back tears. "Yeah, I know. We've been all over this before. It doesn't help." She waved at the door. "Did you see the fun in Nancy's eyes? Feel the joy from her because she's going to get to keep her goddamed cast?"

"Yes, I did."

"Then tell me my little girl will live and grow to be a woman." She turned away and sat in a chair across the room.

"You know I can't tell you that. I wish to God I could. I've known you and Nancy since she was born—I want to say it, but I can't."

"I'm sorry, Charles. Dumping all this on you is inappropriate. I apologize."

"No apology necessary." He opened a filing cabinet and put Nancy's X-rays away. "May I ask you a personal question?" He leaned against the counter and faced her.

"Of course." She wiped her eyes and smiled. "I believe I know where you're going with this."

"How are *you?"*

"I'm fine." She looked away.

"Are you, really?"

"Work is going well. The contractor is finishing up the ramp and gazebo so Nancy can get out and feed the gulls without breaking her neck in the soft sand." She grinned and wiped her eyes. "Yeah, I'm doing okay."

"That's nice. What about *you?"*

"Do we need to go there?"

"As your doctor, I think we do."

"You're not a shrink, Charles." Carolyn

thought of John and the picnic.

"No, but I'm a friend and I care about you."

"I'm flattered." She hesitated and looked around the examination room. "I met a guy." She fiddled with a tissue. "I like him."

"This is outstanding. You're seeing him?"

"We had a date. Well, a picnic on the beach."

"Has he met Nancy?"

"No, but the little brat got a peek at him."

"I'm impressed." Dr. Bailey went to Carolyn and took her hands. "More than impressed, I'm pleased. You need this. Will you let Nancy meet this man?"

"I don't know." She looked up at the doctor. "I'm not sure right now." She squeezed Charles' hands. "Maybe."

Dr. Bailey went back to the counter and picked up Nancy's chart. "I'm pleased. You've found a man."

"A date, doctor. Just a date."

"Let's go to my office before Nancy gets there."

On the way toward the rear of the clinic Carolyn chuckled. "I met John through a mutual friend."

"Did Sandy introduce him?"

"No, it was Timmy a twelve-year-old boy

that I've been running with."

Dr. Bailey opened the office door. "Has the boy met Nancy?"

"Not yet." Carolyn sat in front of the doctor's desk. "I don't really think there's a match there."

"And why not?" He sat behind the desk with a big grin on his face.

"Timmy's athletic. He runs every day, plays in little league, and I doubt he'd be interested in a girl in a wheelchair." She checked her watch.

"You might be surprised."

"His parents are divorced. Poor kid, he misses his dad a lot. Timmy calls John his man-friend."

"Am I talking with the Carolyn Parker I've known for nearly twelve angry years?" The doctor sat back brimming with delight.

"What are you getting at?"

"Carolyn, you've been smiling since you mentioned John and Timmy." He came out from behind his desk and leaned against it.

"So, I smiled, so what?"

"Let me put on my shrink's hat for a moment."

"Will I get a bill?" She laughed.

"You're pleased. More than pleased." He folded his arms. "You're sitting here talking about a man without calling him a sonofabitch. This is the Carolyn I'd hoped to see someday."

"It's no big deal. John is a nice person." She chuckled. "He took me to the Harbor House and was so nervous it was funny."

"And?"

"The man's not a phony, not in the least. I got us out of there."

"No dinner?"

"We went on a picnic instead." She laughed louder.

"A picnic at night?"

"Yeah, on the beach in Coronado. He let me drive his old VW bug and I had a blast."

"You're talking like a twenty-year-old and I think it's wonderful." His phone buzzed. "Yes?" He nodded. "Okay, bring her in."

"They ready?"

"Alice said the cast is off and Nancy's showing it to everybody in the clinic."

"I don't doubt it."

"If you could see yourself right now."

"What?"

"Your eyes are sparkling, You're radiant."

"I'm all that?"

"And more. Carolyn, you've hoped for a miracle. John and Timmy just dropped in your lap. Think about sharing them with your daughter."

"It might be too late. John went back to Texas to see his mother. He may decide to stay there, he's not sure." Her eyes welled. "Dammit—I miss him."

Alice knocked on the open door and wheeled Nancy in.

"Hey, Mom!" She held up her arm. "I'm all human again."

Carolyn went to the child and hugged her. "Why are you crying?"

"They're good tears. I'm happy for you, my little princess."

Innocence lives
in the hearts
of
suffering children

Chapter Thirty
A Sudden Sorrow

EL PASO, TEXAS – 1:00 PM:
A TACO SHOP DOWNTOWN:

John Freeman thought about the note he had left for Susan and smiled. *She'll be pleased and mad at me for writing it.* He looked out from the window booth and watched the people and traffic. *Everybody's going somewhere, I guess and I've got a long way to go myself.*

The din of the restaurant came back into focus. He finished his late lunch and waved at the waiter.

The young man came to the table. "Something else, amigo?"

"Just the check."

"Everything was okay?"

"Yeah, great." John slipped out of the booth and put two dollar bills on the table. "That's for you."

"Thank you signor."

"You're welcome." He went to the cashier and paid.

The pretty Mexican girl smiled. "You have a nice day, sir."

"Thank you, I will." He grinned. "Those pay phones over there working?"

"They were this morning."

"Thanks." He dug some quarters out of his pocket and dropped one into one of the three phones and dialed UCSD.

"UCSD Athletic Department. This is Barbara, how may I direct your call?"

"Hi, Barb. John Freeman here. Let me talk to Dr. Lawrence please."

Silence.

"Barb?"

"I'll put you through to Ned."

A shudder crawled up through John and caught in his throat.

"John, where are you?"

"El Paso." He caught a breath. "Something wrong?"

"We tried to reach you, but there was no number for you in Texas."

"What is it, Ned?"

"Dr. Lawrence passed away Friday evening."

"What happened?" John gripped the phone and remembered. *It was just some indigestion.*

"Heart attack. He slumped over at dinner. His wife called 911, but they couldn't save him."

Silence.

"Where is he?" John's legs went limp.

"Dr Lawrence was a veteran. We held services at Rosecrans this morning. Are you coming back?"

"Yes, that's what I wanted to tell Bob. Give me a minute." He leaned against the bank of phones. "Dear God."

"John?"

"I'm leaving El Paso now. How's Bob's wife?"

"Betty's okay. We're taking care of her."

"Good." He fetched a breath. "I'll be there as soon as I can."

"I'm sorry, John."

"Yeah, so am I." He hung up and stared at the phone. *I'll do it, Dr. Lawrence and that's a promise.*

He went back inside the taco shop and sat at the counter.

"Can I help you, sir?"

"I'd like a good, stiff drink."

"We have beer and wine."

"Beer, I'll have a beer."

"What would you like?"

"You got an ice cold Corona with a lemon?"

"You bet."

"That's what the doctor ordered. Serve it up, my man."

"One Corona on the way."

John's eyes filled. "I found myself, Bob, and I'm gonna make you proud"

"Excuse me?"

"Nothing. Just get that Corona."

Psalm 116:3

The cords of death
entangled me.
The anguish of the grave
came upon me.
I was overcome by
trouble and sorrow.

Chapter Thirty One
Nothing is Easy

BROOKS & ASSOCIATES – SAN DIEGO: CAROLYN'S OFFICE – 11:30 AM:

A young man, wearing a blue uniform, reached in and tapped on the open door. "Lee Wong's Chinese."

Sandy came out of Carolyn's inner office. "Hi, Bruce. Put it on the conference table." She opened her purse and handed the lad a five-dollar bill. "You brought the extra won ton?"

"Yes, ma'am."

"Thanks. You have a good one." She started opening the white bags. "Hey, girl, it's lunch."

Carolyn finished her phone conversation. "I know. I won't skip this one, count on it. Yes. See you tonight."

Sandy set out the plates and napkins. "Steve won't let up on you, I gather."

"I've missed the last two client dinners and he just reminded me of it." She sat at the conference table and spooned some cashew chicken on a plate. "You and I are always seated with single male clients. I feel like I'm on display for the agency." She opened a container of egg flower soup.

"Actually, we are. You know how Steve believes the male clients relate to us more than to our female associates." Sandy took a bite of mandarin duck."

"Yeah, they relate all right. Straight to our boobs and asses." She sipped some soup. "The bastards."

Sandy chuckled.

"You think it's funny?"

"I was just picturing Nancy showing off her cast to everybody at the clinic."

Carolyn grinned. "That little tyke is so happy with the smallest things. I ache for her and she has more grit than all of us put together." She added some rice to her meal. "I told Charles about Timmy and John."

Sandy sat back. "I don't believe this. What did he say?"

"He suggested I introduce them to Nancy."

"Did you tell him that John ran off to Texas?"

"He said I should call."

"I mentioned that. The doctor and I should become a team." She pulled back to the table. "Are you going to?"

"I've thought about it." She took a bite of food. "I'm suffering from the effects of your curse."

"My what?"

"You said I'd find something in John and then he'd be gone. I did and he is." Carolyn took her soup to the service counter and put it in the microwave. "That's what you said and John's now in Texas."

"I remove the spell." Sandy started packing up the leftover food. "Call the man."

"I'm not sure I should."

"Of course you should. Get in touch with him." She smiled and pointed at Carolyn. "If you don't, your ears will turn bright green."

"It's risky."

"You bet it is. Get in touch with him."

"Maybe I should wait to see if he comes back and calls me."

Sandy put the rest of their lunch in the small refrigerator. "Don't let this go. If you feel anything for this guy, do something about it." She washed the two plates and put them in the drainer. "John needs to hear from you."

"If I'm going to have anything with him, he has to come back on his own, not because I ask him to." She removed the soup from the microwave and stirred it. "I'm just not sure."

"I love you like a sister. I care about you and Nancy with all my heart. Do you trust my judgment?"

"You know I do."

"Then listen." She hugged Carolyn. "For the first time in a dozen years you've met a man you like. You even miss him." She stepped back. "Pick up the damn phone and tell him you want to see him again."

"I can't let him meet Nancy."

"No, not right away. Just see where it goes."

"Okay. One call."

"Promise?"

"Yes, I'll make the damn call." They hugged again. "Let's get back to work."

Sandy wiped her eyes on a napkin. "I'm happy for you."

"What about you, Ms. No-guy?"

"We'll tackle that some other time."

"What are you wearing tonight?"

"My red sheath, hair down, fishnets and four-inch red heels." She laughed.

"Steve will shoot you."

"He wants us to relate to clients. I'll be relating."

"Sandy, you're nasty."

"That, I am. Call John."

"I promise."

* * * *

Ten minutes later, Carolyn stared at the note with John's Texas phone number and his mother's name. She took a sip of strong, hot green tea. I can't believe I'm doing this.

* * * *

Sarah picked up on the third ring. "Hello."

"Mrs. Freeman?"

"Yes."

"I'm Carolyn Parker, a friend of your son. May I speak with John please?"

"Oh, my. Sonny left this morning. He's driving back to San Diego. Is anything wrong?"

"No, not at all. If you hear from him, tell him I called."

"He's supposed to call me. I'll tell him."

* * * *

Carolyn stood in the doorway of her office grinning. “I did it.”

Sandra looked up from the folder she was working on at the conference table. “You talked to him?”

“No, his mother. John left Huntsville this morning. He’s on his way back here.”

“You missed him?”

“He’s going to call her. I left a message.”

“This is perfect. I want to hear everything when he calls.”

“He may not.”

“Are you nuts?” Sandy went to Carolyn and hugged her. “He’ll call. Trust me, John will call.”

Chapter Thirty Two
Thunder & lightening

SOUTHWEST NEW MEXICO
LATE AFTERNOON:

John pulled the musty curtain aside. "Shit." Gumball size hail pounded the VW and quickly covered the small parking area of the cheap motel.

Rays of sunlight fought to punch through holes in rolling black clouds. Teeming rain appeared to fall from the angry sky in sheets and forced an 18 wheeler to a stop out on the highway. The big truck's colored lights painted a distorted artwork on the spattered window.

"I can't believe this."

What had been a clear desert afternoon rapidly became a raging airborne battleground. Violent thunder carried John's mind back to Vietnam and drove hot needles into every inch of his skin.

Blue-white fire lit up the swirling folds of black clouds. For an instant, John's frightened image reflected in the streaming, wet glass. He closed the curtain and turned away. The inevitable explosion of thunder rattled the window and pounded against the inside of John's skull. "Dammit!" he shook his head, grabbed the edge of the dresser and sat on the end of the bed.

The lights in the room flickered. He drew a deep breath and caught a look at himself in the clouded mirror. He saw Dr. Lawrence seated on the bleachers at UCSD and heard his mentor's voice. *You have a future here, John ... You have a future here.*

He let the tears come. "I'm so sorry, Bob." He watched the image fade and stared at his own face. "I will be there. I hope to God you can hear me—I will be there!"

He took the phone off the night stand and punched in the area code for Huntsville, Texas. The motel desk clerk answered. "You wish to make a call?"

"I believe that's why I'm dialing the phone."

"I have to plug you into an outside line an' that will be extra."

"Well, sweetheart, you just go right ahead. Plug me in and put the call on my bill."

"I need to charge your card first, sir."

"Charge the damn card and plug in the phone!"

* * * *

It took three rings before Sarah Freeman answered. "Hello."

"Hi, Ma."

"Sonny. Where are you?"

"New Mexico."

A flash of lightening blinked the motel lights and sent a hissing sound through the line.

"What was that?" Sarah hesitated. "Is something wrong?"

"It's a storm. I had to get off the road. I'm in a motel."

"Are you all right?"

"Fine." Another clap of thunder shook the building.

"You're driving?"

"No, Ma. I said I'm in a motel. I'll stay here until the storm passes."

"It's hard to hear you."

"Listen. Do you remember my sponsor at the university?"

Lightening, hissing and a crash of thunder rattled the window.

"Who? Speak up, Johnny."

"Professor Lawrence. The coach I work for." More thunder shook the building.

"Yes, I think so."

"He died, and I'm going to be replacing him. The job is permanent and full time. Tell that to my uncles for me, okay?"

"What happened?'

"Dr. Lawrence had a heart attack and I just found out about it. I've got something solid now. I wanted you to know." John shouted over the clamor of the storm. "Did you hear me?"

"Yes, I heard you. Your uncles will be proud."

"I'm sure they won't."

"What?"

"Nothing. One other thing. There will be a check coming there from UCSD. Put it in another envelope and send it to my La Jolla address."

"I will. Oh. There's a message for you."

"From whom?"

"I got a call from a Carol, I think. She wants you to call her."

"Carolyn Parker?"

"Yes. That's the name, I guess. I just wrote down Carol."

"When did she call?"

Another flash of lightening lit up the room and a rumble of weaker thunder followed.

"It was about two or three hours ago."

"Goddamn."

"You shouldn't take the name of God in vain like you do."

"I know. I gotta go. I'll call you when I get to California."

"You be careful."

"I promise. I love you. I'll call."

"Are you sure you're all right."

"Couldn't be better. Bye, Ma."

A small roll of thunder rumbled in the distance.

John hung up and dialed the Brooks agency in San Diego.

"Would you like to make another call, sir?"

"It would seem so wouldn't it? Charge my card and give me a line!"

"Please hang up, pick up again and wait for the dial tone."

"I will do that. By the way, Ms. That twenty-dollar tip I was going to give you has just gone south."

* * * *

"Brooks and associates. How may I direct your call?"

"This is John Freeman. I'm returning a call to Carolyn Parker. May I speak with her, please?"

"Please hold."

A slight scratching came over the connection.

"Mr. Freeman?"

"Yes."

"I'm sorry. Ms. Parker has left for the day. Is there anything else I can help you with?"

"No. I'll call back tomorrow. Thank you."

John hung up and stared at the phone. Carolyn's voice swam into his head. *I don't know. I'm not sure right now.*

A distant flash of light played across the curtains.

John went to the window and opened the drapes. The setting sun had consumed the remains of the black clouds. The storm had moved on.

Chapter Thirty Three
Client Dinner

SHERATON HOTEL – LA JOLLA, CA:
MAIN BANQUET HALL – 8:00 PM:

Steve Brooks gestured toward the huge screen behind him. "I saved the best for last. You're looking at the state of the art audio/video facilities of Phillips Crown Productions." He nodded at two guests at the head table. "As of three weeks ago, Brooks and Associates has partnered with these talented gentlemen to exclusively create your radio and TV advertising." Steve began the applause and all the guests joined in.

* * * *

Mr. Brooks pointed to a front table near the podium. "My executive and apt client representative, Carolyn Parker and her assistant, Sandy Blair, have been instrumental in this arrangement. You all know them."

Carolyn and Sandy stood and smiled at the crowd.

* * * *

Another round of applause filled the room.

* * * *

Sandy grinned and whispered, "Same old, same old."

Carolyn nodded. "That's why I missed the last two dinners."

A waiter brought a tray of drinks to the table. He nodded at Carolyn. "Red wine?"

"No. I didn't order it."

"The white?" He glanced at Sandy.

She looked across the table. "I told you no more."

One of the two young men said, "I got the scotch with a water back."

The waiter put the drinks in front of him and set the wine on the table. He smiled at the second young man. "And yours would be the martini."

"It would seem so, wouldn't it?" He dropped a dollar on the waiter's tray. "Buy yourself a Rolls."

The server started to walk away. Carolyn opened her purse. "Wait." She handed him a ten-dollar bill. "I apologize for the insult. The man's an ass."

"Thank you." The waiter left.

She glared at the young guy. "What's your name?"

"David. The hostess introduced us."

"I must've forgotten." She pushed the wine away and looked at the other man. "Who are you?"

"Brent Taylor." He took a sip of scotch and chased it with water. "You girls are funny."

"Girls?" Carolyn leaned forward. "You two *boys* are hired table-sitters so it will appear that single women aren't alone at our client dinners."

Sandy cut in. "Sometimes it goes well. This time it doesn't because you two are jerks."

David sipped his drink. "What the hell has you so pissed off?"

"You do, Jungle boy. All through dinner you've been sniffing around imagining what it would be like to get us in bed."

"Don't flatter yourself, lady." He sat back and grinned. "I came for the free meal."

The waiter approached and put crystal bowls of ice cream topped with hot chocolate sauce in front of each of them. "May I refresh your drinks?"

Sandy looked up. "I don't think so."

Carolyn stood, took her white shawl off the back of her chair, picked up the dessert, leaned over the table and dumped it in David's lap. She followed the gesture with the red wine. "That should cool you down."

Sandy got up, grabbed her ice cream and tossed it all over the front of Brent's shirt. "Enjoy your dessert, asshole!"

"You bitch!" He pushed back from the table and started wiping the mess away.

The two women left the banquet hall.

* * * *

Steve had seen the commotion and followed them out to the lobby. "Carolyn, what the hell was all that about?"

"Next dinner, if I decide to attend, Sandy and I won't need paid studs at our table."

"Okay, I'm sorry. I'll take them off the list."

"List?" She put her shawl around her shoulders. "Tear up the list."

"Done." He looked at the two women. "Are you two all right?"

Sandy responded, "We're okay. Go back to your guests."

"We'll talk about it in the morning."

Carolyn looked at him. "No, we won't ever talk about it."

"Agreed. It never happened."

"Thank you." Carolyn waited until Steve left. "Let's get the hell out of here."

* * * *

A moment later, the two women leaned against Carolyn's Mercedes. Sandy pulled a mini-bottle of Black Velvet from her purse. "Want a sip?"

"You're a devil."

"I am." She took a small taste and held the tiny bottle toward Carolyn.

"No, I'll pass." A chilly gust of wind ruffled Carolyn's hair. "Those two assholes made me appreciate John."

"Okay, that's a good thing."

"He's not like them or any of the others."

"This is nice. I like the tone of your voice."

"I believe John is for real." The wind picked up and whipped Carolyn's shawl around her shoulders. "He's on the road. I can't be sure he got my message."

"He'll contact his mom, she'll give him your message and John will call—he will call."

"Thank you for being my friend." Carolyn hugged Sandy. "I'm driving you home."

"I'm okay." She emptied the bottle. "No, I'm not."

* * * *

After dropping Sandy at her apartment complex, Carolyn drove to John's house. She parked in front and walked down the driveway to the side entrance. Pounding waves played their ancient concert and sent ocean wind through her hair.

"I miss you, John Freeman." Her whisper had little strength in the constant song of the sea.

Bright moonlight painted the edges of the surf in shining silver. Moon shadows danced along the sand.

Carolyn saw a ghost of the moment. *Timmy introduced her to John.* "I'm letting you in. Please don't make that become a mistake."

Two glistening tears fell onto her white shawl. A gust of wind flipped one end against her face. She touched her cheek. It was as if John had just kissed her.

Chapter Thirty Four
Anticipation

LA JOLLA SHORES, CA – 5:00 PM:
CAROLYN'S PRIVATE BEACH:

"Just because he didn't call today doesn't mean he won't." Sandy hefted a picnic cooler and a basket of plastic dinnerware. "He's on the road. He'll call."

Late afternoon sun threw long shadows through the newly finished gazebo and onto the solid ramp leading from the house.

Nancy maneuvered her wheelchair over the boards and looked back at her mother. "Are we talking about John, the cute man with the funny car?"

"You just watch where you're going, little girl, and don't be nosey."

"I can't help but hear you two." She struggled to hold her lap full of hamburger buns and potato chips.

"Go on ahead into the gazebo and be careful."

Sandy grinned and handed Carolyn the basket. "She knows about John? You didn't tell me."

"The little busybody got away from Clara when John came to pick me up." Carolyn chuckled. "Nancy went to the front window and saw him. When I found out, I was angry, but for some reason, I'm not now."

The two women stepped into the gazebo behind Nancy. The child had opened the chips and held one out to a hungry seagull. "There you are, Pokey, I have more."

The large gull settled on the wide railing and ate the chip. Nancy gave him another. The bird quickly consumed it. "Now you chew your food."

Sandy put the picnic cooler on a table that had been built against a wall of the gazebo. "You named them?"

Nancy smiled. "I've named them all." She stroked the gull. Pokey turned his head from side to side and *squawked.*

Sandy sat on the bench beside the table. "I can't believe this."

Carolyn joined her. "I couldn't either, but when I saw it, I made the decision to have this ten thousand dollar ramp and gazebo put in."

Nancy gave Pokey another chip. "Look, here come Lucy and Ricky." Two more gulls lighted on the railing. She gave them each a chip. They stayed and ate their treats. "You be good an' I'll have some burger pieces for you later."

Sandy nudged Carolyn. "The birds aren't fighting over the food."

The child petted Lucy. "I told them fighting wasn't allowed."

Carolyn choked up. "I had to do this for her, and I'm damn glad I did."

Nancy stroked Ricky and gave the bird another chip. "Thank you, Mom. I love you." The seagulls *squawked* and flew away. "They'll be back."

Sandy held her emotions. "Are you hungry?"

"I'm gonna eat three burgers, with lots of pickles and a whole bag of chips."

Sandy took Carolyn's hand. "The child is blessed. This is an omen. I have no idea how, but it means something." She took a breath. "Believe me. John is part of this. He will call you, and for God's sake let him in." She hugged Carolyn. "I'm so happy for you."

"I feel it too. I hope I'm not wrong."

Another large seagull landed on the railing and *squawked.* "Look, Mom. This is Chewbacca."

"Who?"

"Chewbacca, from Star Wars, he helped Hans Solo fly the Millennium Falcon." She handed the bird a big chip. "Easy now. Come back later for more." The gull took the chip and flew away.

Both women sat in silence for a moment.

Sandy spoke first. "Let John into your life—all of it."

"I've considered it."

"If he can't deal with Nancy, then he's nothing."

"We'll see. Dammit. It won't happen overnight."

Nancy moved her wheelchair away from the railing. "Are we gonna eat or what?"

Chapter Thirty Five
A Taste of Hope

CALIFORNIA – THE NEXT EVENING:
WESTBOUND INTERSTATE 8 – 4:15 PM:

John had put Arizona and a good chunk of Southern California behind him. He pulled into the Shell station at I-8 and Tavern road. An hour more and he'd be home.

A young attendant walked toward the pumps wiping his hands on a shop cloth. "What'll it be?"

"I get service here?"

"What the hell, I ain't doin' much else."

"Great. Fill it with regular and check the oil, I think it'll take a quart."

"You got it."

"I have to make a call. The keys are in it. Move it if it gets in the way."

"Not a problem."

John went to the single pay phone beside the service bay. He studied Carolyn's business card. "This is it."

"Brooks and Associates. This is Lisa, how may I direct your call?"

"I'd like to speak to Carolyn Parker if I may."

"Whom shall I say is calling?"

"John Freeman."

"Please hold."

He took a deep breath and remembered the picnic on the beach, the wind fluttering Carolyn's hair and the firelight sparkling in her eyes.

"John?"

"Yeah. Hi." A wave of excitement started to build. "You called my mom?"

"Yes, I did." She removed an earring so she could hold the receiver closer. "I just wanted to tell you I had a great time on our date." She hesitated. "Your mother said you were on your way back to San Diego."

"I'm back. Well, I'm about an hour away right now." He paused. "Can I see you?"

She smiled, turned toward the window and looked out at the bay. "Yes, when?" A warm tingle ran up the back of her neck.

"How about tonight?" John held his breath. "I have to get home, take a shower, get dressed, do all that. Can we meet somewhere?"

"No. You do what you have to and pick me up at my place about eight. Will that work?"

"I'll make it work." Another hesitation. "Carolyn, I've missed you."

"Me too."

"Where would you like to go?"

"It doesn't matter, does it?"

"Not really."

"Pick me up. We'll take it from there."

"I'm glad I decided to come back."

She swung her chair around and took a breath. "So am I."

"I'll be there on time."

"See you then, bye."

Sandy stepped into the office. "Yes?"

"We're going out."

"I told you—didn't I tell you?"

Carolyn sighed. "I don't know what to think."

"Don't. Where are you going?

"I have no idea and I don't care."

"This seems so right ... you need this, girl."

Chapter Thirty Six
A Smile & a Tear

BROOKS & ASSOCIATES:
CAROLYN'S OFFICE – 5:00 PM:

Sandy put several file folders on Carolyn's desk. "These are the new projects for the next TV campaigns. All of them have been signed over to Phillips and Crown Productions."

Carolyn held up her hand and spoke into the phone. "Thanks. Lisa, you're a doll." She leaned back and smiled at her assistant.

"Your date with John will mess up the cocktail party?"

"You're on your own with Mr. Phillips and Mr. Crown."

"Steve will have a fit, but I'll cover for you." She sat on a chair in front of Carolyn's desk. "These guys expect you there. I'll think of something."

"I just had Lisa give Steve the message. He owes me from the client dinner."

"So, I'm going to play nice to two men and their wives while you go off on a date." She grinned. "I want to hear every detail tomorrow."

Carolyn pulled her chair up to the desk and leaned forward. "I felt good when John called. All I wanted to hear was him asking to see me." She took a breath and shook her head. "Can you believe that? I wanted him to." She laughed. "I can't believe it myself."

Sandy grinned. "This is great. I'll do the cocktail thing alone. Two married guys and Steve. It'll be a piece of cake."

"Am I going nuts here or what?"

"Yeah, you are, and it's about time."

Carolyn laughed again and spun all the way around in her chair. "I feel happy, Sandy. This isn't me." She hesitated. "What the hell am I getting into?"

The younger woman relaxed and nodded. "I think it's something I'd like to be getting into myself." She got up and checked her watch. "It's knock off time. You go home and get ready for John. I'll get gussied up for a long, boring evening. Nonetheless, my heart will be with you."

Carolyn pushed away from her desk and stood. "Are you upset?"

"Actually, I'm jealous, but you know what? I'm happy for you and I love you." She smiled. "God bless you both."

* * * *

POINT LOMA – SAN DIEGO – 6:00 PM: ROSECRANS NATIONAL CEMETARY:

John had made good time driving in from the East County. He decided to pay his respects to his mentor before going home.

The guard at the cemetery gate handed him a map. "We're closing, sir. You have about a half hour."

"Okay, thank you." He glanced at the paper. "I'm looking for Captain Robert Lawrence. He would be a recent burial."

The guard leaned back into his booth. "The captain was a cremation, sir. He would be in section two-fifty-six along the north wall. You'll have to read the name tags in that area. I don't believe permanent plaques have been installed yet."

* * * *

The setting sun cast long, black shadows to the east of hundreds of white crosses. The image doubled the count.

* * * *

This is a place of sorrow. It's a garden of death for thousands known and unknown who have given everything in their service.

* * * *

John found the north wall and parked nearby.

* * * *

White tags fluttered in the breeze and appeared to be on fire in the setting sun. The ashes of officers and enlisted rested in urns sealed in the long gray stone construction.

An arrangement of fresh flowers rustled in a drab green plastic vase at the foot of the tall rampart. Halfway up, above the cluster of roses, a new tag caught John's eye.

* * * *

CAPTAIN ROBERT LAWRENCE
USMC
1934 TO 1978

* * * *

He stepped back and saluted his departed friend. "I will not—" John's voice cracked. His eyes stung and tears came. "I will never let you down, sir." He reached up and touched the blank surface of the captain's small crypt.

* * * *

The voice of Dr. Lawrence sifted through his head. *Consider your options, John. You have a good future here.*

"Thanks to you, I do." He saluted again. "Assistant coach John Freeman reporting for duty, sir."

Chapter Thirty Seven
A New Start

LA JOLLA, CA:
CAROLYN'S HOUSE – 5:45 PM:

Mrs. Nelson added a tablespoon of fresh garlic to her simmering pot of pasta sauce and stirred. "I made enough for an army and now you're not going to eat."

"Sorry, Clara. I didn't know I had a date until an hour and a half ago." Carolyn continued drying her hair with a dark blue towel. "Besides, I'm too nervous to eat."

Nancy moved her wheelchair away from the television and motored into the huge chef's kitchen. "Can I meet handsome John this time?"

Carolyn tossed the towel over the child's head. "Not tonight."

"When?"

"That's entirely up to me, isn't it?"

"I could die before you say so."

Carolyn drew a sharp breath. "Don't ever say such a thing." She pulled the towel off the child. "Never say it."

JOHN'S BEACH HOUSE – 6:15 PM:

He opened the front windows to let in fresh air. The answering machine was blinking. Three messages were waiting. John pushed the play button.

This is your mother. I hate these things. I have urgent news. Call me right away.

He dialed her number. Sarah answered on the second ring. "Hello."

"It's me, Ma. What's wrong?"

"Sonny, thank God. I could have a heart attack waiting for you to call."

"I just got in. You said urgent."

"Are you sitting down?"

"No."

"Sit down, Son."

He sat on the arm of his worn sofa. "What is it?"

* * * *

CAROLYN'S HOUSE – AT THE SAME TIME:

Nancy watched Mrs. Nelson spoon hot spaghetti sauce over her pasta. "Aunt Clara, why does Mom hide me?"

"She doesn't, child. She just wants to protect you."

"From what?" Nancy twisted up a small fork full of pasta and ate it. "Is John a bad person?"

"Of course not. If he were, your mother wouldn't be seeing him at all."

"Then why can't I meet him?" She took another mouthful of spaghetti, sucked up a stray string. It spattered sauce on her chin and she laughed. "I think I like John. Mom does. I saw them hug and he kissed her."

"That was not for you to see."

"But, I did."

"Yes, and your mother got mad at me because I didn't keep you away from the window."

Nancy swallowed a sip of milk. "Did mom make that awful face when she got mad?"

"I don't think so." Clara fixed a plate for herself. "You have to promise me. When John comes tonight, you'll stay away from the front window."

"I'll try, but I can't promise."

"Nancy, you must not disobey."

"I'll try." She grinned and ate another forkful of pasta.

JOHN'S PLACE – SAME TIME:

He rubbed his face and took a breath. "You're sure about this?" He clutched the receiver and looked around his disarrayed living room.

"Yes, Son. The family lawyer called yesterday. I had no idea your father had done this."

John slipped off the arm of the couch and settled into the soft cushions. "I'm getting an inheritance of five-hundred-thousand-dollars?"

"Yes, Sonny. The attorney has sent the papers to you out there. You sign them and a check will follow."

"I can't believe it."

"It was set up by your papa as soon as you reached your thirty-sixth birthday."

"The old man did this for me?"

"He loved you, Sonny."

"What about you, Ma?"

"I'm well taken care of. The house is paid for and Papa left me more than I'll ever need."

He leaned on both knees. "I'm stunned. I don't know what to say."

"Go to synagogue on the Sabbath. Pray and thank Papa for taking care of us." Sarah choked up. "Are you okay, Son?"

"I'm fine. A little shocked, but I'm okay."

"What about Christine?"

John gritted his teeth. "She'll get what she deserves."

"You'll take care of her?"

"Bet on it, Ma. Chris will be taken care of."

"You'll pray for Papa?"

"I will, promise."

"I love you, Sonny."

"Love you too. It's late there. You go to bed, okay?"

"I'm going to. Goodbye."

* * * *

CAROLYN'S HOUSE – SAME TIME:

Nancy took a bite of garlic bread. "Can I have more?"

Aunt Clara smiled and put another helping of pasta and sauce on the child's plate. "You can have all you want, honey."

"Will I get all big an' fat like the walrus at the zoo?"

Carolyn came in from the dining room, sat At the table and grinned at her daughter. "You're doing a good job on that pasta."

"Aunt Clara said if I didn't eat seconds she'd tie an' gag me and lock me in the hall closet."

"God forbid. I would never say such a thing."

Carolyn said, "You've been watching the wrong TV shows again."

"Well, it would keep me away from the front window." She glared at her mother. "Then, for sure, I couldn't see John or anybody else."

"You're being sassy and telling fibs. I want you to apologize to Aunt Clara right now."

"She was only kidding."

"Doesn't matter. Nancy, I'm waiting."

"Okay .... I'm sorry, Aunt Clara." She wiped her eyes with a napkin. "I didn't mean it."

"I know, child. Finish your milk and we'll have some strawberry ice cream."

"Are you angry with me, Mom?"

"No, sweetheart, I just don't want you to say things that aren't true." She smiled and ruffled the girl's hair. "I think I'll have a taste of ice cream too."

* * * *

JOHN'S BEACH HOUSE – 7:10 PM:

He climbed out of the shower humming a Jim Morrison tune and wiped the steam off the mirror. "You're a good lookin' dude, Mr. Freeman. Thank you very much, Papa."

* * * *

Ten minutes later, John called Christine's gift shop. "Hi, Chrissie. It's your beloved ex. I came back early and I'm staying. I know the shop is closed. I didn't want to get into a phone fight, so I'm leaving a message for you. I'll be in touch soon. Have a great day."

He hung up and smiled. "The next time we get together it will be in the company of lawyers."

He switched on the outside light and locked the front door. He thought of Carolyn and started singing, Roberta Flack's song, The First Time Ever I saw Your Face.

Chapter Thirty Eight
Second Date

CAROLYN'S HOUSE – 7:45 PM:

"You look nice, Mom."

"Thank you, honey." Carolyn adjusted the sleeves on her gray cowl-necked sweater and slipped into a burgundy blazer. "Clara, does this look right with jeans and black loafers?"

"I agree with Nancy." She stood in the archway between the kitchen and the living room. "You're fussing over yourself and I think that's just great."

"Thank you both." She turned around to show off her outfit.

"You're being funny, Mom." Nancy hesitated. "I'm sorry I was bad before."

Carolyn sat on the edge of the sofa in front of the child and held her hands. "You're never bad, angel. Frustrated, yes, but not really bad. We always love you."

"I sassed and told a fib."

"You did and you apologized." She kissed Nancy on the cheek. "You are forgiven and because you're so sweet, Aunt Clara can let you stay up an extra hour."

"That's great!" She cocked her head. "He's here." Nancy turned her chair, went to the front window, pulled the curtain aside. "It's John's funny car."

"Nancy!" Clara dashed into the room and pulled the drape shut.

Carolyn stood, shook her finger at her daughter. "Okay, little girl, we'll let that one slide. Off to your room until we're gone."

"Phooey."

"Now!"

"Yes, Mother."

Aunt Clara stayed by the window. "I'm sorry."

"It's not your fault." She took a breath. "I don't think we'll be too late."

"Not to worry." She smiled. "You just go and have a good time."

"I think I will." Carolyn hugged the older woman. "You're the best."

* * * *

John went around the VW and opened the passenger door. "You are beautiful." He grinned and resisted the urge to grab her and lift her off her feet.

Carolyn didn't hesitate. She went to him, hugged him and kissed him. "I'm so glad you decided to come back." Her eyes filled, she kissed him again. "I missed you and you have no idea how strange that is for me."

He drew a deep breath and held her. "I'm flattered and completely blown away." He shook his head and smiled. "Am I dreaming, or is this Carolyn Parker I'm holding?"

"It's me—a new me and I'm scared to death by it."

He squeezed her and whispered, "I'm trembling."

"I know. So am I."

"If I let go, promise you won't disappear."

"I won't. You promise too."

"I'm here, I'm real. Now more than ever." He pulled back and looked at her. "May I take you out?"

"Absolutely." She kissed his chin.

"Where do you want to go?"

"I don't care. Anywhere."

John gestured toward the VW. "My chariot waits."

Carolyn laughed, dug into her shoulder purse and handed John a set of keys. "We'll take mine."

"The Mercedes?"

"Yes, and you drive."

"I'm impressed. Where is it?"

"Through the gate and into the garage."

"How does the Hotel Del sound?"

"With you, it will be a paradise."

"We're on the way."

"John?"

"Yes?"

Carolyn hugged him again. "I don't want this to be a mistake."

He looked into her glistening eyes. "I promise. I will never hurt you."

* * * *

Nancy came into the hallway. "Are they gone yet?"

Aunt Clara put the dessert bowls into the dishwasher. "They should be by now."

The child moved her wheelchair to the front window and pulled back the drape. "Nope. They're hugging and kissing. Right on!"

"Nancy!"

Chapter Thirty Nine
Second Date Part Two

CORONADO, CA – 8:30 PM:
HOTEL DEL – PATIO LOUNGE:

Candlelight enhanced the movement of Carolyn's auburn hair in the gentle ocean breeze. John smiled and sipped his merlot.

"What?" Carolyn grinned.

"I remember how the fire at our crazy picnic danced through your hair."

"That was a nutty, fun night." She took a bite of iced shrimp. "I felt comfortable with you and believe me, I was surprised."

"By me?" He sat back and studied her, the look of her. The very presence of Carolyn overwhelmed him. *I'm falling in love with her.* The mere thought shook through his heart and fit like a glove.

"Not you." She took a swallow of chardonnay. "By myself. There I was. On the beach, dressed for dinner, feet in the sand eating a deli sandwich, drinking wine out of a plastic cup ... and." She hesitated.

"And what?"

"I loved every minute of it."

"So did I. What's not to love?"

"Nothing—everything." She took a swallow of wine. "I don't know. It just hasn't been like me for a long time."

"I don't usually go on a picnic at night with just anybody either." He leaned forward and ate a cold shrimp. "It was the best date I can remember. That is, until this one."

Carolyn looked at him for a long moment. "I haven't been on an actual date in over eleven years." She took another drink and a short breath. "Now here I am with you a second time."

"I can't believe that."

"What?"

"Eleven years without a date." He caught the waiter's attention and held up two fingers.

"I have issues, John, and lots of baggage."

"Everybody has baggage. I have a ton of it myself." He gestured toward the crowd on the patio. "All these folks laughing, talking and enjoying themselves, they're loaded down with baggage. So what?"

"What about a child?" Carolyn caught herself. She saw Nancy in the gazebo with the gulls.

"A kid? You mean Timmy?"

The waiter brought two more glasses of wine and put them on their table. "More shrimp cocktail, sir?"

John nodded at Carolyn. "Yes?"

"Okay."

The server said, "Coming right up."

"Timmy isn't baggage. We both love him. You mentioned, on the way here, that he can't wait for the three of us to run together again." He dipped a big shrimp in sauce and ate it.

"He makes us a threesome." She sipped some wine. "You're okay with that?"

"Of course. How could that be a problem?"

"Most of the men I've encountered can't deal with something like Timmy. They want me alone, no encumbrances, no commitments."

He reached across the table and took her hands in his. "I'm not like those guys." He studied her face. "I can handle whatever baggage comes with you."

Carolyn pulled a hand away, picked up a shrimp and munched it. "Are you sure?" She smiled. "Are you really sure?"

"Trust me."

"I hate it when someone says that." She swallowed a drink of wine. "I'm serious."

"So am I. More than you know."

"I think I can believe you."

"You can."

"That's what's scaring the hell out of me."

"Why, because I'm not a flake?" He leaned back and ate a shrimp. "I have feelings for you, Carolyn."

"No kidding." She smiled and touched his face. "Don't you think I know that?"

He took her hand and kissed it. "Most of the reason I came back was to be with you." He watched her eyes brighten.

"I'm flattered, and you know what?"

"No, what?"

"You haven't made one gesture or move to get in my pants."

"I wouldn't do that." His face lit up and he pushed back from the table. "I just can't act like that."

"Why?" She drank more wine. "Wouldn't you love to?" She watched him fill with embarrassment.

"This is inappropriate."

"Answer me. Every guy I've had the unpleasant occasion to be with wants to get me in bed. Why not you?" She ate another shrimp and waved at the waiter.

"You said you haven't dated in eleven years."

"Business dinners, clients. They're not dates."

He sat forward and whispered, "I come from the old school, Carolyn. It has probably crumbled to dust by now, but I believe in its teaching."

"And that is?"

The server came to the table. "More for you both?"

John nodded. "Yes, and some coffee please." He looked at Carolyn. "Would I like to get your wonderful, sweet ass in bed?" He took a swallow of wine. "Bet on it." He drained his glass. "I'm not like your salivating clients. I would require your permission first. Until I had that, nothing would ever happen."

She raised her glass. "You are the exception."

He dipped a shrimp in cocktail sauce and bit into it. "Why did you bring sex into our conversation?"

"I wanted to know how you'd respond." She leaned forward, took his hand and pressed it to her face. "I'm very pleased."

"Okay, I'm glad you are." He smiled, lifted his glass and nodded. "Thank you."

Carolyn grinned and clinked her glass against his. "By the way, you have my permission."

"I appreciate that." He looked at her and sipped his wine. "Can we take a walk on the beach?"

"I'll get sand in my shoes."

"Take them off. I'll carry them."

Chapter Forty
Second Date Part Three

HOTEL DEL CORONADO - 9:30 PM:
THE BEACH – A FEW YARDS WEST OF THE HOTEL:

Carolyn stumbled and hung onto John for support. "Almost lost it."

"You okay?"

"Yeah. Walking in stocking feet isn't all that easy."

The constant opera of the surf grew louder. Chilly ocean wind blew through Carolyn's hair. John held her closer. "You warm enough?"

"I am with you."

"That's a compliment. Thank you." He held her and listened to the song of the waves. "Carolyn, you're special."

"Am I now?" She looked up at him. "What makes you say that?" Light from the hotel patio shined in her eyes.

He held her tighter and pressed her head against his chest. "You. Just you. The scent of you. Everything there is about you." He looked out at the black sea and inhaled a breath of salt air. "We spoke about baggage earlier."

"Yes. I have a lot of it." Carolyn pulled back and looked at him.

"Well, here's mine." He kissed her on the forehead, her nose and on the lips as gently as a soft spring breeze. "I have an ex-wife."

"You told me that." She hugged him. "It's okay."

"Just listen." He smiled and kissed her again. "Christine is baggage that will soon be gone forever." He pushed a lock of hair out of her eyes. "I promise you that."

"How does she matter?" A gust of wind tossed her hair back over her face.

"She mattered yesterday, but not anymore." He hugged Carolyn and laughed. "Not anymore."

"Make sense, John, please."

"I'm sorry." He squeezed her. "Let's sit down here." They sat in the sand and he cuddled her to him. "I'm coming off like a nut, I know."

"You are, and I'm about ready to call for help."

"I'm two months late on my rent and that's history." John held her close and rocked her.

"Where are you going with all this?" Carolyn pulled away and stared at him.

"On my way back from Texas I got hit with a shock." He fetched a breath and looked out at the surf.

"What happened?"

"My boss at UCSD, Dr. Robert Lawrence, my mentor, died while I was back home."

Carolyn looked at him and saw the pain in his eyes. "I'm so sorry."

"Bob had a heart attack. He was in his late forties. It shook me to the core." He held her in silence for a moment. "I'm going to fill Bob's position as assistant coach of the track team."

Carolyn touched his face and kissed him on the right cheek. "I don't see that as baggage." She snuggled closer.

"I promised Dr. Lawrence I wouldn't let him down."

"Good, you have a solid future."

"It will consume ninety-eight percent of my time."

"Great, we'll have the other two percent to be together." She caught a breath and stared out into the rolling waves.

He leaned back on both elbows, grinned and stared up at the stars. "Did you hear what you just said?"

Carolyn moved closer and pulled at the lapels of his sport coat. "I don't want you to catch cold."

"Are you listening?" He got up on one elbow and pushed a lock of hair out of her eyes. "You just—"

She pressed a finger to his lips. "Let it be."

He sat up and looked at her shadowed face in the dim light from the hotel patio. "You're beautiful. I'm filled with you and I'm—"

She touched his lips again. "Just let it be."

Silver light from a quarter moon found its way through scattered clouds and shined in Carolyn's smiling eyes.

Chapter Forty One
Looking Back

UCSD – LA JOLLA, CA – 8:30 AM:
OFFICE OF ASSISTANT COACH DR. ROBERT LAWRENCE:

John's throat tightened when he looked into the large oak trophy case. A year-old picture of the track team gave him a sad smile. He and Coach Lawrence stood in the center holding a big gold cup.

The moment fell from the back of his mind and blurred his vision. *We did it, John. Our guys took the finals.*

"I don't know how yet, Bob." He blinked the photo into focus. "But, I'll tell you what—we'll do it again."

"He was a good man."

John turned. "Sorry, sir, the door was open."

Alex Ross, the athletic director, smiled and held out his hand. "It's your office now." They shook hands.

"Coach Lawrence was the best and I'm privileged to have worked with him." A chill worked its way across the back of John's neck. *I'm chatting with the top gun here.*

"Bob had a lot of confidence in you. He sold your abilities like he was recruiting you from Notre Dame."

"Coach Lawrence was a dear friend, sir." He walked toward the big desk and nodded at the chair. "I promise you, I'll work as hard as I can to fill that seat."

"From what Bob told me, I believe you will." Alex stepped forward and shook John's hand again. "Take your time getting settled. In honor of Professor Lawrence the team won't resume training until Monday. His psych classes are off until next semester." He started toward the door. "The head coach will help you with anything you need. You know Ned?"

"Yes, sir."

"Welcome aboard, John."

"Thank you." He eased himself into the assistant coach's chair and glanced around the office. *This is a major step into your future.*

Don't screw it up. An image of Carolyn slipped into his head and painted a big smile across his face. "I can't mess up—I will not."

* * * *

CAROLYN'S HOUSE – ONE HOUR EARLIER:

Clara cleared away the breakfast dishes. "You want more coffee?" She started rinsing the plates.

Nancy swallowed a gulp of orange juice. "I'll have a cup with two sugars and fresh cream, thank you."

"You're funny." Carolyn pinched her daughter's right earlobe. "No, Clara, I have a meeting with Steve and Sandy this morning and I'm running late already." She reached down and tickled Nancy's ribs.

The child giggled. "Stop, Mom. You know that makes me lose my breath."

The older woman looked at Carolyn and smiled. "I love to see this."

"What?"

"Look at you." She wiped her hands on a dishtowel. "You're radiant. You're full of something and I think I know what that is." She opened the dishwasher and started loading it.

"I feel good for a change."

"I'll say." She finished putting in the

knives and forks.

Nancy drank the rest of her juice. "I saw you and John kiss an' hug last night and that's why you're so happy this morning."

Carolyn stared at the child through a stern expression. "Okay, smarty-pants, naughty little girl. Why did you break the rule again?"

Nancy moved her wheelchair away from the table and started to cry. "Because I care, because I wanted to see you and John together!" She shook her head back and forth. "I'm sick of being a secret."

Aunt Clara stepped away from the counter. "It was my fault."

Carolyn raised her hand. "It's all right." She took a napkin off the table and handed it to the child. "Wipe your face."

"You're not mad at me?" Morning sun played through the kitchen window and highlighted Nancy's long brown hair.

"No, I'm not mad. I'm ashamed of myself." She knelt beside her child's wheelchair and hugged her. "I am so ashamed."

"Can I meet John?" Nancy grinned. "Can I?"

"Yes you can, when the time is right, and that will be soon." She hugged the child again. "I'll see to it."

Clara blotted her eyes on the end of her apron. "Thank the Lord." She took a breath.

"Thank the Lord."

Carolyn kissed Nancy on the forehead. "Look what's happened to my makeup." She kissed her on the cheek. "You go to your room and work on your studies. I want to talk with Aunt Clara."

"I love you, Mom."

"Me too. Go on now. I'll see you after work."

"I can't wait to meet John."

"You will, now scoot."

Clara sat at the kitchen table. "I tried to keep her from the front window."

Carolyn patted the older woman's hand. "That doesn't matter. I need to ask you something." She glanced toward the counter. "Did you dump the coffee?"

"No, but you're late."

"The hell with it, I'll have a half cup."

"Me too." She got up and fixed two fresh cups. "What is it?"

"I never poked my nose into your private life, but I'd like to know about your marriage."

Carla put the coffee on the table and sat down. "My late husband and I had forty-seven good years." She smiled and looked out into the room. A warm glow came over her face. "We had two sons. They moved on. Neither have had children, that's why I love your Nancy so much.

She's like a grandchild to me."

"I know that and I'm pleased by the bond you have with her." Carolyn stirred sugar and cream into to her coffee. "What I'm asking is …." She sipped from her cup. "How did you make it through forty-seven years?"

Clara smiled. "I know this is about John."

"It is." Carolyn took another sip of coffee.

"We got through all those years with belief and trust in each other. We kept no secrets. My Michael was my life. He was always there for me." She touched Carolyn's arm. "I gave him my heart and he treasured it." She sat back and looked at Carolyn. "Is this John of yours that kind of man?"

"I can't be sure, but I think he might be."

Nancy slipped back from the hall. She went into her room and quietly closed the door. The child's face beamed with excitement. "I'm gonna meet John."

Chapter Forty Two
Taking Action

UCSD – LA JOLLA, CA – 10:00 AM:
JOHN'S OFFICE:

Head Coach Ned Sully tapped on the open door. "May I come in?"

John was in the process of arranging his desk. "I guess so. You're the boss."

"I had this made up for you." He handed him a long thin cardboard box. "I think you'll like it."

John opened one end of the carton and pulled out a polished cherry wood name plate. "I haven't earned this yet." He smiled and admired the gift.

Assistant Coach
John Freeman

"I am honored. Thank you." He shook Ned's hand. "I hope I can live up to it."

"We're all sure you will. Bob believed in you and that's good enough for us." He gave him a manila envelope. "It's from administration. Read it over, sign the papers and you become a fulltime employee of the university."

"I'm overwhelmed." He put the envelope on the desk and set the name plate in place.

"When you wade through all that paperwork, you'll find a nice raise."

"I owe all this to Dr. Lawrence, you and the director. I will not let you down."

"We know that, John. If there was any doubt, you wouldn't be here."

"Thank you again."

"Get settled, do what you want with the office, just put it through me." He started to walk away. "Oh, there's a faculty luncheon tomorrow at twelve-thirty. You're the honored guest."

"I can't believe this."

"The university is paying tribute to Professor Lawrence and we want to welcome you to the department. Write up a speech." Ned smiled. "Wear a coat and tie."

"A speech?"

"Keep it light." He gave thumbs up. "See you there."

John watched Ned leave the office and stared at the open door. "Me, an honored guest?" He studied the name plate on his desk. "Write a damn speech?"

* * * *

BROOKS & ASSOCIATES – ONE HOUR EARLIER:
CONFERENCE ROOM – CAROLYN'S OFFICE:

Sandy came in ahead of Carolyn and put a stack of files on the table. "Okay—I want to know what's up."

"What's up?" She went to the service bar and got a cold bottle of water. "Should there be something up?"

"Don't be coy. All through that meeting you were smiling and agreeing with everything Steve said." She slapped the top file. "He just dumped six new clients on us and you took it all in stride." Sandy sat at the table and opened the top file. "What the hell's going on with you?"

"I'm going to do it."

"Do what?"

"I'm letting John in. He's going to meet Nancy."

"You're kidding me"

"I've decided to introduce John to Nancy. Or is it proper the other way around?"

"Carolyn—I'm excited, ecstatic and scared to death."

"So am I." She took a long drink of water. "You've been pushing me to do it, now I'm ready." Streams of mid-day sun reached in through the vertical blinds and caught the sparkle in her eyes. "Now it's time."

"What brought this on?" Sandy leaned forward and crossed her arms on the conference table. "It's not like you."

"We went out last night."

"Date two. How did it go?" Sandy grinned and waited.

"He's sincere and I trust him." Carolyn took her empty water bottle to the service counter and tossed it in the trash. "You said it yourself, if he can't handle Nancy, he's not worth a damn."

"I did an' I meant it." She pushed her chair from the table. "When will this event take place?"

"I'm not sure, but soon."

* * * *

UCSD – LA JOLLA, CA 1:30 PM:
JOHN'S OFFICE:

He dialed the number for a civil attorney.

"Selman, Greenburg and Goldman. May I help you?"

"I need to propose an alimony settlement."

"Mr. Greenburg handles those cases, sir."

"May I speak with him please?"

"Mr. Greenburg is not available by phone. You'll need to make an appointment for a consultation."

"Okay, let's do that."

"He's open at eight-thirty tomorrow morning. For whom shall I make the appointment? "

"John Freeman."

"Do you have the address?"

"Third and Broadway, fourth floor, suite 424."

"Correct. We'll see you then."

"I'll be there." He hung up. Christine came to mind. *You have to take care of me, John. That's just the way it is.* He smiled. "Think in terms of *was,* Chris. Past tense. You're about to become history."

Chapter Forty Three
Winds of Change

JOHN'S BEACH HOUSE – 5:00 AM:

"C'mon, lazy, we're ready to go." Carolyn laughed and ran in place.

John came out on the porch and pulled his sweatshirt over his head. He spotted the boy. "Timmy!" He jumped down onto the sand, grabbed the kid and lifted him off his feet. "Hey, champ. I'm back." He hugged him and set him down. "I've missed you, big guy."

Carolyn smiled and leaned on her thighs. *This is so right.* The thought crept through her like a warm August breeze.

Timmy hugged his man-friend and pulled back. "Are you staying?"

"You bet—and we're gonna do lots of stuff." He ruffled the boy's hair. "You like the San Diego Padres?"

"Are you kidding?" Timmy's smile shined in the faint predawn light. "I pretend I'm one of them every time I play ball."

"Have you seen them play?" He glanced at Carolyn and grinned.

"No. My mom can't afford to take me to the games."

"Would she like to go to the stadium?"

"She watches the games on TV."

"Tell you what, champ." He leaned down and held the boy by the shoulders. "I just happen to have access to season tickets for a party of four." He smiled at Carolyn again. "How would you and your mom like to attend every home game this season?"

"She wouldn't be able to."

"The three of us then. Carolyn, you and me. How's that?"

"It would be the greatest thing ever."

"You got it, big guy. Consider it done."

Timmy hugged John. "You're the best." He looked up at his man-friend with tears in his eyes. "I'll have to get my mom's permission."

"Somehow, I don't think that'll be a problem." He looked over at Carolyn. "How can you be so beautiful at five in the morning?"

She threw her arms around him and squeezed. She kissed him. “You’re a special man, John.” She shook her head. “I think I’m ....”

He put a finger to her lips. “Remember what you said?” He kissed her forehead. “Just let it be.”

Timmy started jogging in place. “You guys are cute.” He smiled at them. "Are we gonna run or what?”

Early light pushed through the fog and played across the waves and onto the silver sand. John shouted, “Go ahead, we’ll catch you.”

“I doubt it.” Timmy took off north along the surf.

John studied Carolyn’s face for a moment. “I have an appointment downtown at eight-thirty so it’ll be a short workout.”

“How was your first day back at the university?”

“Scary to say the least. I have to address a luncheon today and that’ll be a first.”

“You’ll do fine.”

They started trotting behind Timmy. John took Carolyn’s hand. “You up for dinner tonight?”

“Another picnic?”

"Tom Hamm's. I'll make up for my failure at the Harbor House." He bumped her hip, knocked her off balance and she fell onto the soft sand.

"You did that on purpose."

He lay down beside her and pushed strands of hair away from her face. "Yes, I did." He kissed her. "Dinner tonight?" He helped her up.

"I'd love to." She brushed sand off her shorts.

"I'll swing by at seven-thirty."

"That won't work. We have a late session at the agency."

"Okay, what's a better time?"

"Can you get reservations for 9:00?"

"Not a problem. I'll be at your place at eight-thirty."

"Better yet, I'll come right from the office and meet you there."

"Sounds like a plan. I'll be waiting in the lounge."

Carolyn adjusted the bauble on her ponytail. "Know what?"

"I can't imagine." He held her and kissed her forehead.

"You just earned about a thousand points with me."

"How did I do that?"

"By the way you acted with Timmy and the offer to take him to baseball games. Not just one time, but for the entire season. Do you have any idea how happy you made him?"

"Indeed I do. That's why I did it." He grinned. "I get a discount through the university."

Carolyn stepped back and looked at him. "I can't believe you."

"It's true and I'd like you to go along."

"I know you meant it and the gesture touched me more than you can imagine."

"I love the kid. He's a buddy." He smiled. "Besides, Timmy brought you into my life."

"I'm pleased about that too." A flock of seagulls flew off the ocean and landed nearby. Carolyn smiled at the thought of Nancy feeding the birds in the gazebo.

"What is it?"

"I need to ask you something."

"I'm all ears."

Timmy yelled from a distance, "Hey, you guys comin'?"

John waved. "We'll be right there." He nodded. "Your question?"

"What if that lovely boy weren't athletic and maybe couldn't run with you or even play baseball?" She swallowed hard.

"That's how I got to meet him. If it was some other way and he couldn't do those things, it wouldn't matter to me. He'd still be Timmy Collins. Why are you asking?"

"I have never, ever, met a man like you." She strained to keep from grabbing him and hugging the breath out of his lungs. "You're too good to be real."

"Why, because I like kids?" He waved at Timmy again. "We'll be there." They started a fast walk in Timmy's direction.

"You're amazing."

"Nope, just me." He laughed. "I love all kinds of children. I'll have to introduce you to my favorite group sometime."

"Group?" They picked up their pace.

"You ever hear of Angels Unaware?"

Carolyn stopped in her tracks. "My agency sponsors a fund raiser for them every year." Her throat tightened. She drew a long breath of chilled ocean air. Goose bumps crawled up her bare legs and arms.

John stopped a few yards ahead of her and looked back. "Got a stitch in your side?"

Her voice cracked. "What about those children? They're all mentally challenged."

"I do volunteer projects with them every other month." He laughed. "They're the sweetest little people on earth."

Carolyn started to cry. "You work with those kids?"

"Yeah, I do. What's wrong?"

"Nothing—everything is perfect." She could hardly say the words. "You're perfect." She ran to him and held him. "You are so perfect."

"If you think so, that's okay by me."

She kissed him and squeezed harder. "We'll talk more about all this at dinner." She looked up at him. "I'm so pleased with you."

"Thank you very much." He pulled up the end of his sweatshirt and wiped her face. "Tonight at Tom Hamm's." He studied her face for a moment. "Why are you crying?"

"I'm not crying, John—I'm soaring."

Chapter Forty Four
Freeman vs. Freeman

**SAN DIEGO – 3rd & BROADWAY:
SELMAN – GREENBURG & GOLDMAN – 8:00 AM:**

"Good morning, Mr. Freeman. You're early."

"I thought it would be a good idea."

"Mr. Greenburg will be impressed. I'll tell him you're here." She pushed a button on her console and smiled. "John Freeman is here." She held out her hand. "I'm Terri O'Malley. I hope we can be of service."

He shook the lady's hand. "Thank you." *An Irish redhead at the front desk of a Jewish law firm?*

"Mr. Greenburg will be with you in a moment."

"I don't mind waiting." *I can imagine Greenburg. Short, dressed in an Armani suit, wearing Italian loafers and puffing on a Corona cigar.*

John stood by the front window looking down on Broadway and the hustle/bustle of the city's morning. *I wonder how much chaos I'm in for.* He heard a pleasant chime from Terri's area.

"I'll send him in." She looked up from her desk. "Mr. Greenburg will see you now."

"That was quick."

"We don't keep our clients waiting."

He heard a *clack.* "Which door?"

"The center one, to your left."

"Thank you." He walked to the door and entered an elaborate, spacious office. *This is going to be expensive.*

"Mr. Freeman?

"Yes."

The voice came from an open door to the right of a huge cherry wood desk. "Be with you in a second."

"That's fine." He looked around at the high-end furnishings. A giant portrait of a stern-looking gentleman adorned the wall behind the desk. *That's got to be Greenburg.*

A young man about John's age came out

of the room and approached. "Okay, let's get started." He had the smile of a movie star. “I’m David.” He extended his hand. “That old guy on the wall is my dad. He owns the firm.”

John shook the man’s hand. “A pleasure, sir.”

“David, please. May I call you John?”

“Yes, of course.”

“Have you had breakfast?” David wore an open-collar white shirt, a light blue cardigan, tan slacks and what appeared to be imported dark brown loafers.

“Just a cup of coffee before I left the house.”

“Good, we’ll have something.” He gestured toward a chair in front of the desk. “How about some warm pastry and great French coffee?”

“That would be perfect.”

David pressed a button on his desk phone. “Terri, did we get fresh rolls this morning?”

“We sure did.”

“Have Bonny bring in a tray and a pot of my fave coffee.”

“On the way.”

The attorney looked at John. “You seem perplexed.”

"I didn't expect to be treated like a long-term client."

"Let's hope we can enjoy such a relationship."

"Excuse me, but I'm a bit scattered by all of this."

David smiled and took a notepad off his desk. "Let me put it to you straight."

"Please do. I just want to propose a settlement to my ex-wife."

"Of course, that's why you're here." David sat down across from John. "Christine is into you for a thousand a month and she's petitioned her lawyer for two-hundred-fifty more."

"How the hell do you know that?"

"John, your divorce records and alimony payments are a matter of public record. When you made an appointment to propose a settlement, I had my people run a complete check."

Bonny came in with a tray of hot coffee and warm pastry. "Where do you want it, David?"

"Here, on the coffee table."

John waited while the woman poured coffee into two cups and left. "You checked me out?"

"I have to know what's going on with you

before I can represent your case." David put sugar and cream into his coffee.

"Am I going to be charged for this investigation? I haven't agreed to anything yet."

David drank some coffee. "It's part of the package. Should we not come to terms, there won't be any charge."

"And if we do?"

"Relax, John. Enjoy your coffee." He stood and pressed the intercom.

"Yes, sir?"

"Good morning, Sally. Bring in my standard settlement and billing forms please."

"I'm on it."

"I'll give you a breakdown on how all this process works." He made a note on a yellow pad.

"David, I don't mean to be difficult."

"You're not. I want you to be comfortable with what lies ahead."

A clack sounded from the office door. Sally, a smartly dressed young blonde, walked in carrying two file folders. She smiled at John and handed the files to the attorney.

"Thank you. I'd like you to meet Mr. Freeman. He may be a new client."

John stood and shook her hand. "It's my pleasure."

"You've picked the right firm."

David smiled at the woman. “Thank you, honey.” She left the office with the glide of a fashion model.

John sat down. “She’s very nice.”

“Sally’s my wife.” David opened one of the folders.

A wave of heat ran up the back of John’s neck. “Sorry.”

The lawyer grinned and held up a sheaf of forms. “These are all the hoops we have to jump through to create a solid settlement offer.”

“It’ll take me a month to fill all that out.”

David laughed. “Every client says the same thing.” He handed John the papers. “Just glance over it. All you have to do is sign the forms. If we come to an agreement today, my people do all the legwork. The proposal will be ready for your approval Friday morning.”

“Do I need to read it now?” He leafed through the fifty-page document.

“Not unless you want to. I have no intention of screwing you, John.”

“I didn’t think that.” He handed the papers back to the attorney. “I’m just a little out of my element here.”

“Understandable.” David handed him the second folder. “That is a complete assessment of our basic charges for a settlement petition. You keep those papers for your records.”

He opened the folder and looked at the cover page. “Jesus. Five hundred for the pre-investigation. A thousand dollar retainer and you get a hundred-fifty for each hour billed!” He sat back and closed the folder. “I’m sorry, you’re out of my league.”

David smiled and poured more coffee for both of them. “Easy. You’re a Vietnam vet, right?”

“I am.”

“We’ll drop the retainer fee.” He looked at John through a sincere expression. “I admire you. At the time of that horror, I was in second year law at Harvard. I didn’t think I was privileged. My father saw to it I was kept out of the draft.” He took a sip of coffee. “I felt guilty.”

“Admirable.” John shifted in his chair.

“You’re on staff at UCSD.”

“I’m an assistant coach.”

“I studied pre-law there while you were crawling through jungles and swamps.” He smiled. “Forget the investigation charges.” He picked up a cheese Danish and bit into it.

“Why would you do this?” John drank some coffee.

“Because I want to.” He smiled. “We’re also of the same faith and I take that seriously.”

"I appreciate your gestures. What's the bottom line?"

"Let's cut hours billed to a hundred bucks each. Sound good?"

"Are you kidding me?"

"Not for a second." He swallowed more coffee. "Have we got a deal?"

John reached out and shook his hand. "Let's do it."

David grinned. "Good. Your package will top out between fifteen-hundred and two-thousand."

"I can handle that. What's next?" John spread cream cheese on a sliced bagel.

"Now we get into the nitty-gritty." David went around his desk, opened a drawer and came back with a tape recorder. "The rest of our session needs to be on tape."

"Why?"

"Everything you tell me must be documented in the event we have to take the case to court."

"I thought we'd just send the petition to Christine's lawyer and wait for a response."

"I wish it were that simple, but it isn't." He put the recorder on the table. "Everything you tell me goes on the tape. I'm the only one in this office who will have access to it except Sally. She'll transcribe it, print two copies. You get one, we keep the other."

"This is for the court?"

"If it goes that far."

"I don't understand."

"Court, we don't want. However, we have to be prepared for that event."

"Okay, I'm a dummy. If not court, what?"

"Here's how it works." David added more coffee to his cup and took a small bite of Danish. "Once the papers are filed, we send the petition to Christine's attorney and set up an arbitration hearing."

"A hearing?"

"Yes. You and I and Christine's lawyer have to sit face-to-face across a table before an arbitrator."

"Chris will be there?" He took a short breath.

"She will, and she'll be less than pleasant. I guarantee it." David took another bite of Danish. "If you're lucky, she'll sneer at you and accept the settlement."

"If she doesn't?"

"We take her to civil court and then it gets messy."

"I'm prepared to offer her ten-thousand dollars in two payments. How can she turn that down?"

"Do the math, John. Christine gets more than that per year now and she's seeking an increase. The lady's running a good game."

"You got that right." He bit into his bagel. "The bitch has been strapping me every month and I want out from under."

David drank more coffee. "Does she have other income?"

"Christine owns a gift shop. Before the divorce the business was grossing around sixty-thousand a year. I think its double that now."

"We'll find out for sure." The lawyer made a note. "One more thing before I start the tape. "You're having trouble with the alimony now. Where is the settlement coming from?"

John smiled. "If I tell you that, you'll cancel the discounts you gave me."

"I really need to know. In a case like this, I don't want any surprises during litigation." He topped off his coffee. "It doesn't go on the recording or beyond this office." David grinned. "It won't change our agreement."

"My father established a trust fund for me that neither my mother nor I knew about. I turned thirty-six recently and the trust was released to me." He swallowed some coffee. "I've just become five-hundred-thousand-dollars richer."

David sat up straight. "Have you

deposited those funds?"

"No. The papers are in the mail. All I have to do is sign and return them to the family attorney."

"When you get the check, don't deposit it."

"Why?"

"Listen to me carefully." He stood and leaned against his desk. "Christine doesn't have to know."

"She hasn't a clue. I was going to offer her the ten grand flat out. Then, I decided to get a lawyer."

"Consider that to be the best move of your life."

"I'm in the dark here."

David walked all the way around his desk, came back and sat down. "This changes our approach."

"How? I'll have the money. I can cut her a check, you make it legal and Christine is off my back."

"John, if she finds out about your inheritance, she can tie your settlement offer up in the system. She could, and probably would, eat at you for years."

"Now what?" He took another bite of cold bagel.

The lawyer tapped his notepad then made

an entry. He looked over at John. “Where do you bank?”

“Wells Fargo.”

“When you get your check, do not deposit it in that account.”

“I’m not following.” John poured more coffee from the silver service.

“How much is in your checking account right now?”

“Roughly three-thousand after my UCSD bonus clears.”

“Open an account in another bank. I suggest a high-interest savings account.”

“Where do I get the money for a settlement?”

“You don’t. We’re not proposing a settlement.”

“What the hell *are* we doing?”

“How much do you make a year?”

John rubbed the back of his neck. “With my dad’s college endowment and the GI Bill—”

“Those don’t count. Christine can’t touch them an’ they’re not considered income. What’s your UCSD salary?”

“I paid taxes on twenty-six-thousand-five-hundred last year.”

“No other income?”

“None.”

"You can't afford the current alimony, much less the two-hundred-fifty increase."

"I can now."

"Christine doesn't know that." David wrote more notes. "Forget settlement. We're going to get you off the hook altogether."

"You're a miracle worker?"

He chuckled. "No, I'm a sharp attorney. If Christine's gift shop is bringing in the money you say, she's earning more than double what you are. She should be paying you alimony."

"I'll buy that."

"We won't go there. It isn't necessary."

"Obviously, you're way ahead of me. Where the hell do we go?"

David grinned and took a bite of pastry. "I'm glad you came to this firm. I love cases like this." He swallowed some coffee. "My people will find out how much Christine is earning with the gift shop. We'll have that information by the close of business today."

"That quick?"

"It's a no-brainer, John. Then we file a show cause order and her attorney is bound, by law, to respond."

"Show cause for what?"

"They have to prove that your ex needs your monthly support." He smiled. "With the money she's making and what you're earning, she doesn't stand a chance of winning." He held up his coffee cup. "You'll be off the hook."

"Just like that?"

"Be aware, Christine's lawyer will file for and get your bank records. That's why you must put your inheritance check in a separate account. When the dust settles, Christine can't touch you."

"Do we get into her accounts?"

"We have the same option and I assure you, we'll exercise it." David picked up the tape recorder. "By the time we get to arbitration, Christine will be cut off at the knees."

"I don't really like the image of that."

He leaned forward. "Nether do I, but it's time to get her off your back."

"Yes, it is."

"Okay, I'm going to start the recording. You answer accordingly to everything regarding your income and your current financial situation. Is that agreed?"

"Yes."

"John Freeman, what is your salary as an assistant coach at UCSD?"

"Approximately twenty-six-thousand-five-hundred-dollars a year."

"How much money is in your checking

and/or savings account as of this date?"

"About three thousand five hundred dollars."

Chapter Forty Five
The Time is Right

CAROLYN'S OFFICE 11:45 AM:

Sandy opened the foil covers on the hot containers of Italian takeout and put plates and utensils on the conference table for herself and Carolyn. "I've opened a bottle of merlot to go with this lunch."

"Great." Carolyn came out of her office and headed toward the service bar. "We'll have it in glasses, not Solo cups."

"I'm for that. This is a celebration, girl." She used two forks to put linguine with white clam sauce on the two plates. "You want grated cheese on yours?"

Carolyn came back to the table with two

wine glasses. "Lots, please. She sat down and poured the wine. "I still can't believe it."

"I can't either." Sandy took a forkful of pasta. "If John actually works with Angels Unaware, then meeting Nancy is the best thing for the three of you."

"And you."

"Me?" She took a generous sip of wine. "How do I fit?"

"You've been my dearest friend since Nancy was born." Carolyn reached across the table and squeezed Sandy's hand. "I want you there when she meets John."

Sandy took another sip of wine and wiped her mouth on a napkin. "You've been putting this together all morning, right?" The younger woman leaned back and grinned. "Carolyn Parker, you're shameless."

"I have a perfect plan." She smiled and drank some wine.

"You've been cooking this up while I've been working on our new accounts?"

"I'm guilty."

"What's the plan?"

"Can you be at my place for a Saturday cook out?" She grinned and sipped merlot.

"Yes. What's up your sleeve?" Sandy sprinkled more cheese on her pasta and grinned.

"When I have dinner with John tonight, I'm going to invite him over." She leaned forward. "I want you to be there and I'm going to ask John to bring Timmy."

"The boy you've been running with?" She took a breath. "You want Nancy to meet both John and Timmy?"

"Yes. It's time and I'm sure of John." She gulped a swallow of wine. "I'll invite him and Timmy to meet some friends."

Sandy poured more wine in their glasses. "If Steve knew we were consuming a bottle of wine at lunch he'd be furious." She grinned. "Today, it's necessary."

Carolyn laughed. "He's doing a three martini lunch. What's the difference?"

"I'm going to be blunt."

"About what?"

"When you have dinner with John tonight, quiz him about what he does with the kids at Angels Unaware. If it doesn't equate with what we know about their programs, then he's a phony."

"You want me to interrogate him?"

"Just ask the right questions. If he's for real, you'll know it."

"I hope to God he is."

"If he isn't, I'll castrate him with a dull knife."

"I'll hold him down."

They both laughed.

Sandy tore off a piece of garlic bread. "You're going to the restaurant right from here?"

"I've changed my mind." She smiled and finished her wine. "I'll beg off early and go home to freshen up and change."

"That's a great idea. I'll cover for you at the meeting and make some excuse to Steve."

"I love you, Sandy. You're the most wonderful friend anyone could ever hope to have."

"You too, girl. I just want to see you happy."

"Thanks. I have a good feeling about tonight."

* * * *

CAROLYN'S HOUSE – 8:15 PM:

She walked into the living room. "How do I look?"

Aunt Clara and Nancy were watching a Disney movie on TV and laughing.

Nancy turned her chair away from the television. "Wow! Mom—you look like a movie star."

Clara got up off the sofa. “You haven’t worn that red dress and those gold heels in over two years. You’re stunning.” Clara stepped closer. “Turn around.”

Carolyn turned left then right. “I need to look special tonight.”

Nancy moved her wheelchair closer to her mother. “John will pick you up an’ carry you off to his castle.”

“I don’t think he has a castle.” She sat on the sofa and handed her daughter a pair of earrings. “Could you help me with these?”

“You want me to poke them through the holes?”

“Please, sweetheart. I’m too shaky right now.”

Clara smiled. “I’m so happy for you.”

“Thank you. We’ll see how it goes.”

“Hold still, Mom.”

“Sorry.”

Nancy pushed the wire through her mother’s left earlobe. “That’s one. Turn your head.”

She kissed the child’s cheek. “I love you.”

“Mother, if you don’t stop moving I’ll be piercing another hole in your earlobe.” She put the right earring in place, leaned back and grinned. “Done. Those are my favorites. I love the way they dangle and sparkle.”

"Thank you, honey." Carolyn's eyes filled. "When you get older, I'll let you wear them." She took a breath. Her voice cracked. "We'll have to drill holes in your little earlobes of course."

"No way! I'll go for the screw-on kind."

Aunt Clara laughed. "They just put a cork behind your lobe and poke a needle through it."

Nancy cupped both of her ears. "Not mine—yuck!"

Carolyn looked at the older woman. "Is my makeup okay?"

"You're beautiful."

"You always are, Mom."

"Thank you both." She leaned forward and took Nancy's hands in hers. "I have a great big surprise for you. Actually, a double one."

"I'm going to meet John?"

"You're such a smarty." She looked up at Clara and smiled. "Yes. We're going to have a barbecue Saturday. John and Sandy are coming. We'll have Aunt Clara's great potato salad, hamburgers and hotdogs and you'll get to meet John."

"What's the other part?"

"That's the big secret." She touched the child's face with both hands. "I'll make this happen for you."

"Promise?" Nancy moved her chair back. "You really promise I'll meet John?"

Carolyn got up off the sofa and adjusted her dress. “John and his funny yellow car will be here on Saturday.”

“An’ what else?”

“Don’t push it, little girl. That’s the surprise.” She leaned down and kissed her daughter on the forehead. “Go watch the rest of your movie. I want to talk with Aunt Clara before I leave.”

“Tell John I think he’s handsome.”

“I’ll be sure he gets the message.” She went into the entranceway and took a blue scarf off a rack by the front door. “This look okay?”

“Carolyn, I’ve never seen you so nervous.”

“I’ve just promised my daughter something I may not be able to deliver. I never should’ve done that.”

Clara hugged her. “If this John is what he seems to be, you’ll fulfill your promise to Nancy.”

“You’re sure I look all right?”

“You look like a goddess. If he can’t see that, he’s blind.”

Chapter Forty Six
What Will Be, Will Be

JOHN'S BEACH HOUSE:
TWO HOURS EARLIER:

The remains of the setting sun ignited the distant horizon. Orange flames reached through the carport and railings of the porch. The house appeared to be on fire.

He climbed out of his VW and grabbed several hangers of dry cleaning from the hook behind the driver's seat. He squinted into the sunset and watched the long, moving shadows of a flock of seagulls and sand pipers along the edge of the surf.

I'm glad I decided to come back here. He took the clothing and his gym bag inside.

The blinking red light on the phone caught his attention. "Now what?" He pressed the play button and draped his dry cleaning over the sofa.

Hi, John. This is David Greenberg. We got the information on Christine's gift shop. It's good news. The lady's doing quite well. She paid state and federal taxes on a gross of one-hundred-fifteen-thousand. Her personal income came to ninety-three-thousand and change. Christine enjoyed a refund of twelve-thousand-six-hundred. In addition to all that, her house was paid off last year. She can kiss your alimony goodbye. We file the show-cause order on Friday. I'll be in touch. Relax, John, it's in the bag.

"Yes!" He punched the back of the sofa. "Yes!" He picked up the dry cleaning and headed for the bedroom. "Thank you, David."

* * * *

TOM HAM'S LIGHTHOUSE 8:50 PM:

John nursed a glass of chardonnay and kept an eye on the front entrance. An attractive brunette approached. "Mr. Freeman, your window table won't be available for another half hour."

"That's okay. Thank you." He adjusted his tie for the third time. "My date isn't here yet."

A couple walked in from the foyer and behind them stood Carolyn. John waved. *Oh my God. She's gorgeous.*

She spotted him and came into the lounge. John got up and nearly knocked over his wine. He stepped away from the small table and took her hand. "Our booth will be ready in about twenty minutes or so." He pushed the table out and they sat down. "What would you like?"

"An ice cold margarita." She adjusted her scarf. "How'd it go with the speech?"

He caught the waiter's attention. "It was an experience for me. I couldn't write a speech. I gave that up."

The waiter came to the table. "What can I get you?"

John pointed to his glass. "One more chardonnay and the lady would like a margarita."

Carolyn smiled. "Straight up, please and no salt."

"Got it. I'll be right back."

"So what did you say?"

"I stood there, looked out at all those professors, and told them what a wonderful man Dr. Lawrence was and how he made a difference in my life." He looked away. "It was the truth. I didn't need any kind of speech."

She patted his hand. "The truth always works."

The waiter came back with their drinks and put them on the table. "Your window booth will be ready in about fifteen minutes."

John put a five on the young man's tray. "Thank you."

Carolyn squeezed John's arm. "You look nice."

"Me?" He sat back and finished his wine. "Lady, when I saw you walk into this room I went numb. You take my breath away."

"I hope not." She smiled and let her hair fall forward over one shoulder.

"Believe me, you do." He reached up and touched her left earring. "Everything about you is beautiful."

The waiter returned with more drinks. "I'm sorry for the delay on your window table. We always have a problem with that. Everybody wants to be seated there and there are only so many available. This round is on the house."

John held up his hand. "It's not a problem. Can we take our drinks to the dock while we wait?"

"Of course. I'll have the hostess tell you when your table's ready."

"Great, we appreciate that." He put another five on the waiter's tray. "C'mon, lady." He took Carolyn by the hand. "Off to the floating dock we go."

* * * *

Another couple went by. John nodded and held Carolyn's arm. "I'm sure you've been here before." They stepped onto the moving dock. "It's like getting on a small boat."

Carolyn got her balance and leaned against the outer railing. "Yes, I've been here, but not in such pleasant company."

He studied her face for a moment and handed her his glass. "Warm enough?" He adjusted her scarf and took back his wine. "There's so much I want to share with you."

"I want to hear it all." She sipped her drink. "May I ask you something?"

"Anything."

"What do you do with Angels Unaware?" Carolyn watched his eyes.

"A lot of fun things." He took a drink of chardonnay.

"I mean, specifically." The dock moved. She leaned against the rail and held eye contact.

"They're such innocent kids. I wish I could spend more time with them."

"What are the events you get involved with? My agency funds a few. Which ones do you like?"

"There are three every year I try to be part of."

"John." She stiffened. "Please tell me what those are." She moved away from him and took a drink.

He looked at her and smiled. "Is that so important right now?"

"Yes, it's very important."

"Okay. My favorite program comes up in about two weeks."

She nodded. "And that is?"

"Why are you so intense?"

"What's the event?"

"A bunch of students from my track team, with me in charge, of course, take the kids to Sea World." His eyes sparkled and he drew a big smile. "We've made arrangements through the university to rent two big busses and we haul those little angels out for a full day." He finished his wine. "You wouldn't believe the joy on all those innocent faces when they get to meet Shamoo and watch all the shows." He choked and swallowed. "Then we set up the June outing. All the little ones get to go to the San Diego Zoo. That's another full, wonderful day. There's about fifteen of us. We put the kids in double strollers and take them through the entire park." John was filled with excitement as he continued. "I have to admit, a real thriller is taking the angels to the Del Mar Fair—"

"Stop!" Carolyn started to cry. "That's enough." She put her glass on the railing, rushed to him and hugged him. "I'm so sorry."

"What?" He held her. "Why are you upset?"

"I doubted you."

"I don't understand."

"I didn't believe you actually worked with those kids."

"Why would I lie about such a thing?"

"I don't know. I have no idea what I was thinking." She pulled back and looked up at him. "Can you forgive me?"

"For what?"

"For not trusting you."

A gust of wind blew in from the bay and the dock rolled on a wave. John reached out just in time to rescue their glasses from the railing. "Those would be on the bill."

Carolyn blotted her eyes on the ends of her blue scarf. "I must look terrible."

"Lady, if you look terrible, then terrible has a new meaning." He kissed her and squeezed her tight.

"I'm sorry." She wiped her eyes again.

"Are you free on Saturday?"

"For you, yes." He stroked her hair and kissed her forehead. "I'm positive something special is happening here."

She touched his lips. "Remember our rule? Let it be."

"Okay. What's with Saturday?"

"I'm having a barbecue and I want you and Timmy to come over. There are some people I want you both to meet."

"Sounds great to me, but I don't know about Timmy."

"We'll run with him in the morning and invite him. I'm sure his mom will agree."

"Ms. Parker, you're an amazing mystery."

"Not for much longer."

The hostess came out on the top step. "Mr. Freeman, your window table is ready."

John gestured toward the stairs. "Let's go have a great dinner."

Chapter Forty Seven
Handle With Care

JOHN'S OFFICE – 9:00 AM:

"Christine left the message on my phone this morning and she's angry. I thought it best to call you before I respond."

"That was wise. As your attorney, I advise you to be nice and tread easy. Not telling her you had returned from Texas doesn't mean anything. However, her demand for the late payment does. You owe her for the balance of this month, right?"

"I gave her half before I left."

"Okay. Here's the deal. You have to call Christine today. If you don't, she might file a show cause order on you. We don't need that problem."

John got up from his desk and looked out onto the athletic field. "Do I cut her a check?"

"You don't have to. Our show cause will be filed Friday morning. Tell her you're putting a check in the mail today."

"She's heard that before." He watched two runners on the track. One in a yellow jersey, the other in green. *Who would beat whom? My guess is Mr. Green.*

"Take it easy, John. Once our order is filed, Christine's hands are tied. Her lawyer will follow through and he'll be in touch."

"Excuse me, David. I double-checked the petition for the alimony increase. Christine's attorney is a woman."

"Oh boy. Actually, all that means is more intimidation from their side of the table."

"I hope you're right." He laughed. "I can hear the sharpening of knives."

"You have a great sense of humor. Just tell her what I suggested. Call her right away—and be nice."

"I'll do my best." John hung up and saw the young man in green cross the finish line first. *I picked the winner.*

* * * *

BROOKS & ASSOCIATES – 9:30 AM:

Carolyn and Sandy came back from a morning meeting with the sales staff. Sandy said, “I can’t wait for the barbecue.” She held the door for her boss and followed her into the office. “I think I’ll come late and let you guys get together first.” She put her notebook on the conference table. “I don’t want to give John and Timmy too much to deal with at once.”

Carolyn went to the service bar and poured a cup of coffee. “I’ve thought about that.” She nodded toward Sandy. “You want some.”

“Half a cup.” She eased into one of the chairs, pushed back and stretched. “Timmy and John are going to be faced with meeting Nancy, dealing with you and nervous Aunt Clara.” She pulled up to the table. “I should kind of slip in about an hour later.”

“By that time, Timmy and John might be long gone.”

“From what you’ve told me about last night’s date and Timmy’s excitement this morning, I don’t think so.”

Carolyn brought two cups of coffee to the table. “I hope to God you’re right.”

“I don’t know where it’s coming from, but somehow, I think you’ve picked two winners.”

* * * *

John hesitated on punching in the last digit for Christine's gift shop. *If you'd like to make a call, please hang up and dial again.*

"Shit." He dialed the number again and took a breath.

"Chrissie's Boutique, may I help you?"

"Hi. I'd like to speak with Chris please."

"Who's calling?"

"Her ex. I'm returning her call." *Be nice.* He remembered David's advice.

"Just a minute." *Click.* John was on hold listening to scratchy instrumental tunes from the sixties.

Keep your cool. Play it easy.

"John?"

"I'm responding to your call."

"Well, that's just great. Why the hell didn't you let me know you were back?"

"I'm doing it now." He gritted his teeth and held a breath.

"I called your mother and she said you'd left Texas days ago. You're an ass, John. I want my money."

"The check went out yesterday. You'll have it on Friday." He looked out the window. No runners were running and the marine layer was starting to blot out the late morning sun.

"I damn well better. I have a house payment due and business expenses to meet. You're causing me stress."

"I apologize. I'm doing my best right now."

"Your best is usually a day late and a dollar short." She lowered her voice. "What brought you back so soon? You told me you might stay there."

"Things changed."

"What, John? What changed?"

"Dr. Lawrence passed away while I was in Huntsville."

"I'm sorry about your loss. What's that got to do with anything?"

"Thanks for the sentiment, Chris." The fever in his ears came quick. *Let it alone.* "I'm filling his position."

"That means a raise doesn't it?"

"I signed the contract, and yes, I'll be making more money."

"Good, then the alimony increase won't be a problem." She chuckled. "It's about damn time you did something with yourself."

"You know, I really agree with you." He smiled. *Be careful what you say.* "Things have changed for the better. Now, I can take care of you the way I should have two years ago."

"You sound sincere. I like that tone."

"Oh, I'm sincere, Christine, and it feels great. From now on, you won't have to worry about the alimony check being late and that's a promise."

"I'll have to see it to believe it."

The light on the athletic field grew brighter. John turned to face the window again. "I've learned a few things lately and I'm taking action."

"I think I'm pleased with this new attitude. Maybe we could see each other."

"You have my word. We'll see each other real soon."

"Let me know when."

"Count on it." John grinned and sat back in his chair.

"I have to go."

"Me too. Take care." He hung up. "Things are about to change."

* * * *

Several beams of sunlight cut through the clouds and brushed across the surface of the playing field. The day had just become a lot brighter.

Chapter Forty Eight
Order to Show Cause

CHRISTINE'S BOUTIQUE:
FRIDAY 10:00 AM:

"Anita."

The young Spanish girl turned away from the display case at the front of the shop. "Yes, ma'am?"

"Come here." Christine pointed to a wall of glass shelves. "I thought I told you the scented candles are to be arranged at eye level and then down two shelves only."

"They are."

"That's your eye level. You're short. See where I'm standing?"

"Yes."

"What shelf am I looking at?"

Anita looked up. "The fifth, I think."

"You think?" Chris shook her head. "Try not to. Get a step stool and rearrange the candles."

"Christine," Judy, the assistant manager called from the rear counter, "your lawyer's on line one."

"I'll take it in my office." She went around the counter into her office and closed the door. Chris pressed the blinking button. "Hello, Arlene. What's up?"

"Are you sitting down?"

"Yes."

"Your ex has hired an attorney and filed a show cause order."

"Filed a what?"

"We have to show that you need the alimony."

"That sonofabitch!" She looked out into her shop to see a group of tourists making expensive purchases. "John told me everything was fine. Is he fighting the increase?"

"Hold your breath, Chris. John wants the alimony stopped altogether."

"Can he do that?"

"If we can't prove you need the money for support, I'm afraid he can."

"Block the order. Put a stop on it."

"I can't do that. We have to go to arbitration."

"Tie him up in court."

"We can't do that either. A hearing is required. I'll subpoena his bank records and we'll go from there."

"What are my options?" Chris noticed another line of customers at the front counter.

"Unless John has come into a serious amount of money, your options are limited."

"Can you find out?"

"When we get his bank records, I'll know more."

"I'll call that bastard and read him the riot act."

"Chris, listen to me. Do not contact John in any way. Everything from here on involves litigation. That's my expertise, not yours."

"He played me. He told me I wouldn't have to worry about alimony anymore. That sonofabitch was laughing up his sleeve."

"Christine, we both know you've been riding a gravy train for more than two years. I think that train has come to the end of the line."

* * * *

CAROLYN'S HOUSE – FRIDAY – 3:30 PM:

"Can I have some of those beans?" Nancy finished drawing two seagulls on the construction paper. "They smell so good, I'm drooling."

Aunt Clara took the cover off the crock-pot. "I think we can manage that." She got a small cup out of the cupboard. "The beans aren't really done yet. They have to cook for about thirty more minutes." She spooned a small portion of beans into the cup. "You tell me if they need more brown sugar or molasses."

Nancy drove her wheelchair up to the kitchen table and ate a spoon of beans. "They are marvelous."

"Thank you, child." Clara covered the cooker.

"Aunt Clara?" Nancy licked her spoon.

"What is it?"

"Do you think John will like meeting a crippled kid?"

The Rose

The flower is always
tender and soft to the touch.
Some say love is a rose
that can leave your heart to ache.

Chapter Forty Nine
Another Option

UCSD – FRIDAY 4:00 PM:
JOHN'S OFFICE:

The head coach got up to leave and shook John's hand. "You ready for Monday?"

"A little nervous. I have some pretty big shoes to fill." He glanced at the picture of Dr. Lawrence and the track team.

Ned picked up his briefcase and leaned on the back of the chair. "The professor believed in you and you need to know the rest of the faculty was quite impressed with your speech at the luncheon."

"It wasn't really a speech. I spoke the truth about a dear friend and mentor I admired."

"Bob's spirit is here, John, and he'll be on that field Monday morning." He started toward the door. "Study the background I gave you on the new student. He's got the legs of a gazelle." Ned stopped. He's a science major. Go figure. Have a good weekend."

"Thank you, I will." John went to his desk and picked up the file Ned had left.

His phone buzzed.

"Yes?" He sat down. "I'll take the call." He put the phone on speaker. "Hi, David. It's ten after four on a Friday and you're still at the office?"

"I'm one of the few attorneys who think clients are more important than golf."

"I appreciate that." He swung his chair around and enjoyed the western section of the campus.

"You have another option."

"We're gonna hire a hit man to take out Christine?"

"I love your attitude, John." David laughed.

"You've helped me with that."

"Christine's lawyer, Arlene Hamilton, got the show cause order this morning and she's frantic."

"She wants to take the case to court, right?" He turned around and stared at the phone.

"No, she doesn't even want arbitration."

"I don't understand. I thought we had to do that."

"We're all people, John. There are many ways to peel the apple." The attorney hesitated. "Your ex has been less than up front with Arlene."

"Why do I know that would be true?" John pushed his chair away from the desk and watched the patterns of shadows falling across the athletic field.

"I've known Ms. Hamilton since law school. She's a stand-up attorney. That's why she contacted me right away."

"What has the wonderful Christine done?"

"Actually, it's a fine line. At the time of the divorce, your ex petitioned for and got the thousand a month alimony. You didn't contest it and the court confirmed the amount."

"I could've stopped that?"

"If you fought it, you could've gotten the amount reduced."

"So, I've been over-paying for more than two years?"

"Exactly. And that brings us to the point of my call."

"David, I'm totally confused."

"Okay, listen. Ms. Hamilton got access to your bank records the same way we found out about Christine's finances. She immediately realized that your ex was taking you for a ride. Adding the petitioned two-hundred-fifty increase would be nearly criminal."

John rubbed his chin and looked back at the phone. "So now what?"

"Arlene doesn't want arbitration or court. Knowing what she's learned would implicate her in questionable ethics."

"What's the other option?"

"We file a full lawsuit against Christine for total retribution of the nearly thirty-thousand you've paid her."

"I can do that?" He looked out the window and the images blurred.

"You can and it's your call."

"I would get it all back?" He remembered the nasty phone calls and throwing his last check on the coffee table. He heard the venom in her voice when she had called him an ass.

"There are two sides to it, John."

"And they are?"

"We file the suit. That makes it official. Christine has to respond."

"Then what?" He wondered, *do I really want to be so vindictive?* "I'm not sure."

"Okay, I hear you. You're a good person. The other side of the coin is heads and it works in your favor."

"I'm listening." A chill crawled up the center of John's back and bit like a tick behind his ears. *I'm about to take serious legal action against the woman I once loved.*

"The lawsuit puts Christine in a tight corner. She doesn't want all her finances brought out in open court. She damn well doesn't want to have to pay back all the alimony. She'll go for the alternative."

"And that is?"

"Her attorney will advise her to cease and desist on the current alimony and you're off the hook."

"No more payments?"

"None."

"You can do this?"

"If you agree to the filing of the formal retribution suit, Arlene will make Christine well aware of what must be done."

"Then it will be over?"

"Yes, but you won't see any payback on the alimony."

"I think I can live with that."

"Then, I have your permission to file the formal suit?"

"I trust you, David. Do what you think is best."

"Okay. We file Monday, I'll send you the papers. You sign and send them back and Arlene and I will deal with Christine. Know what?"

"What?"

"That woman deserves to be cut off at the knees."

"I still don't like that image." John shook his head and shuddered.

"Will you be okay with all of this?"

"Yes. An' thank you for going the extra mile."

"You're welcome. I have to call Arlene and bring her up to speed. You have a great weekend."

"Thanks, you too."

John closed the call and heard the echo of his mentor's voice. *You earned the win because you worked hard enough to get it.*

Chapter Fifty
Saturday Morning

CAROLYN'S HOUSE – 8:30 AM:

"You look sexy, Mom."

Carolyn slipped into a denim jacket over a pink turtleneck sweater. "Thank you. I don't think sexy would be appropriate."

Nancy grinned. "Those designer jeans and white sneakers sure are."

"Where do you get all these adult observations?"

Aunt Clara put a second piece of French toast on the child's plate. "From the television, where else?" She looked at Carolyn. "You want breakfast?"

"Just some coffee. The sooner I get to the office, the sooner I get back."

"Mom, today is special. Why do you have to go to work?" Nancy poured maple syrup on her toast and added a spoon of powdered sugar.

"I have to meet with Steve. I'm not going to work."

"You're going to the office—that's work."

Carolyn pinched her daughter's left earlobe. "I'll be home in plenty of time for the barbecue and that's a promise." She pinched harder.

"Okay—that hurts!"

"Good." She kissed the child on the cheek. "I wouldn't do anything to spoil this day for you. You're going to meet John, and Aunt Sandy will be here too."

"What's the other surprise?"

"If I told you, it wouldn't be a surprise now would it?" She drank some coffee and got up from the table. "Clara, I'd like a word with you out by the car."

"Of course." Clara wiped her hands on her apron.

Nancy cut a piece of her French toast. "Another secret meeting I'm not supposed to hear."

Carolyn shook her daughter's ponytail.

"Finish your breakfast, little girl, and get ready for the big event."

* * * *

Clara held the door while Carolyn slipped behind the wheel of the Mercedes. "You're flustered, I can feel it."

"I'm scared to death. If anything goes wrong today, I'll never forgive myself."

"It will be as it will. I believe you've made the right choice for yourself and Nancy." She patted Carolyn's arm. "I know you're not religious, but if you trust in the Lord, he'll see you through."

"You're one of the sweetest people I've ever met." She pushed the button and the garage door started opening. "I often wonder how nice it would've been if you were my mother."

"Now, Carolyn, you're going to make me cry."

"Keep Nancy busy and out of mischief." She put the car in gear. "Two hours tops and I'll be back to help."

JOHN'S BEACH HOUSE – 9:15 AM:

"Who's that evil elf knocking upon my

door?" He laughed.

"It's the kid that can outrun you any day."

"C'mon in." John rinsed his cereal bowl and put it in the dish rack. "You ready for a great day?"

"Having a whole Saturday with you an' Carolyn is the best." Timmy stood by the kitchen table. "Do I look okay?"

"Well, let me see. New sneakers, jeans and a UCSD sweatshirt. I'd say you're dressed for the occasion."

"My mom said you called while I was in the shower."

"I wanted to be sure your mother was cool with everything." He dried his hands and sipped some cold coffee. "You seem a little nervous."

"It's the first time I'll be with you guys for a whole day." He pulled a chair from the table and sat down. "Did Carolyn tell you about who she wants us to meet?"

"Not a word. It's all a surprise and she's enjoying keeping us in suspense."

Timmy smiled. "I like her a lot."

"So do I. If only you knew."

"I know."

"Smart kid."

"Yeah, kind of."

"I'll give her a call and see if she wants us to bring anything." He grabbed the phone and punched in Carolyn's home number.

CAROLYN'S HOUSE – 9:30 AM:

Nancy headed toward the patio door when the phone rang. "I'll get it. It's probably mom."

"Nancy!" Aunt Clara put down a large bowl of potato salad. "You know the rules." She rushed into the living room.

"It's time I started helping anyway." She picked up the receiver on the second ring. "Hello—I mean, this is the Parker residence."

Clara got there too late. "Oh … Nancy."

John hesitated. "Is Carolyn there?"

Clara whispered, "Give me the phone."

Nancy turned away. "No, she isn't. Who's calling please?"

"This is John Freeman."

Clara whispered again. "The phone, child. Please."

"Hi John. I'm Nancy—here's Aunt Clara." She held up the receiver and smiled.

Clara glared at her and shook her head. "I'm sorry, John. Carolyn had to go into the office. She should be back in about an hour."

"Not a problem. I just wanted to know if I should bring anything."

"I don't think so."

"Okay, we'll see you a little later." He hung up.

* * * *

"That was strange."

"What?"

He looked at Timmy. "I believe I just spoke with two of the people we're going to meet today." He hesitated. "One of them is a young girl named Nancy."

"Now, I *am* nervous."

"So am I." He got up off the couch. "Let's go. I want to pick up a bottle of wine and then we'll head over to Carolyn's for the big cookout."

Chapter Fifty One
One Step Closer

**BROOKS & ASSOCIATES – 10:45 AM:
STEVE'S OFFICE:**

"Thanks for coming in this morning." He got up from his desk and walked Carolyn out to the lobby. "You and Sandy make my job one hell of a lot easier."

"We love what we do and that makes all the difference."

"So, today's a big day for Nancy?"

"She's excited and I'm suffering acute apprehension."

"That's understandable. This is a major step for you and her."

"Not Nancy. She thinks the circus has come to town and is setting up on our beach." She frowned. "If the big top comes crashing down, I'm afraid my little girl will be deeply hurt."

Steve unlocked the front door. "You know, I believe Nancy has a lot more wisdom than you might think."

"I hope you're right." Carolyn checked her watch. "I told Clara I'd be home in two hours and I'm running late."

"That's my fault. Get going and tell Nancy I'm happy for her."

"Thank you for caring."

"Tell me all about the party on Monday."

CAROLYN'S HOUSE – AT THE SAME TIME:

Clara walked behind Nancy along the ramp to the gazebo. "Go slower, child, before you have another accident."

"I can handle it." She buzzed ahead and pulled up to the table. "Are you still mad at me?" She put the packages of hamburger and hotdog buns on a bench beside the built-in gas grill.

"No, not really mad, just a little peeved."

The woman puffed a breath and set the huge container of potato salad on the bench. "You know the phone rules."

"Yeah, but you had your hands full an' I was closer so I answered." She moved her wheelchair to the other side of the table. "Spread out the cloth and I'll help you get it straight." Two seagulls perched on the far railing.

Clara shook out the checkered tablecloth. "Those birds will be after the food."

Nancy caught the end of the cloth and pulled it down over the end of the table. "That's Ricky and Lucy. They have manners."

"Since when do seagulls have manners?" Clara secured her end of the cloth over the edge of the table.

"I taught them not to fight over their treats and to be polite." She took two small crackers from the pocket of her blouse and held them out to the gulls. Each bird took a treat and waited for another.

Clara shook her head. "Child, you're amazing." She placed the container of potato salad in the center of the table.

* * * *

John parked in front of Carolyn's house and grabbed the bottle of wine. "Let's go see if she's home yet."

Timmy stared at the front entranceway, the French windows and the perfect landscaping. "Wow. She lives here?"

"You haven't seen the place?"

"No. This is a mansion."

"I've been here twice, both times at night. I've never been inside." He got out of the car and walked to the front door. Timmy followed. John rang the doorbell. "She said an hour." He checked his watch. "That's about now."

No answer.

Timmy said, "Maybe they're out back."

"Could be. Let's check."

They walked around the house to a back gate. John saw the open patio door. "Hello. It's John and Timmy. Anybody there?"

"She has a private beach. They could be down there."

"Okay, Champ. We're expected, so it's not like trespassing."

* * * *

Nancy fed the two gulls a second cracker each. "Don't be pigs now. I'll have more for you later." The birds flew off. She turned to Clara.

"You want me to go up to the house and get the cooler?"

"It's too heavy for you. I'll get it."

"See, I'm trying to help an' you won't let me."

"Nancy, please don't make a fuss."

"Well, Mom's late an' Sandy's not here either. How am I going to meet John without a formal introduction?"

Clara opened the cupboard under the table and brought out plastic plates, knives and forks. "You can help by fixing the table while I get the cooler."

"There's somebody coming." Nancy moved her chair out away from the far railing.

Clara turned to see two figures walking down the ramp. "Oh my."

John smiled. "We're early, I hope that's okay."

Nancy drove her chair around the table, out of the shadows and into the bright entrance of the gazebo. "Hi, John. I'm Nancy. My mom's late." She smiled wide and held out her hand. "I'm pleased to meet you." She offered her hand to Timmy. "And who is this other young man?"

Chapter Fifty Two
A Moment of Pause

He felt the burning in his ears and knew his face was flushed. He shook Nancy's hand. "I'm Timmy." The boy glanced at John. "I run with your mother an' Johnny."

Nancy grinned. "I'll bet you're the surprise my mom's been teasing me about."

"I don't know what that means, but I'm pleased to meet you."

She backed her wheelchair away from the gazebo entrance. "John, you're even cuter up close."

"I don't know what to say." The sting in his eyes forced him to blink rapidly.

Nancy gestured toward the interior of the gazebo. "C'mon in out of the sun, we'll chat until

until mom gets here."

John looked at Clara. "Are you okay with this?"

"Mr. Freeman, I believe everything's going to be just fine." She smiled. "I have to bring down a few things from the kitchen."

Timmy stopped staring at Nancy. "Can I help?"

"That would be very kind, young man, thank you."

John put the bottle of wine on the table and watched Nancy move her wheelchair toward the rear of the gazebo and the open screen. "I had no idea your mother had a daughter."

"She wants to protect me because I'm crippled."

John swallowed a burning lump in his throat. "You're a lovely little girl. How old are you?"

"I'm eleven going on twelve." She grinned. "How old is Timmy?"

"He's twelve." He forced himself to hold back his emotions.

Nancy patted the bench next to her. "Come sit."

A large seagull flew in, *squawked* and perched on the railing near the child.

John sat back startled.

"It's okay. This is Chester." She dug a

cracker from her pocket. The bird favored one stiff leg and cocked its head from side to side. "Chester, I want you to meet my new friend, John Freeman." The gull blinked, munched the treat and flew away. "I named him Chester after the Dennis Weaver character on Gunsmoke." She smiled. "He's only one. There are many more that come to visit. I feed them all."

"I'll bet you have names for every one of them." He cleared his throat.

"Oh, yeah. A few of them have trouble remembering who they are, but I know them by sight." She started to close the screen. "If I leave it open, they'll keep flying in."

"That's okay." His voice cracked. "I'd like to meet them."

"Really?" She beamed and slid the screen all the way open. "Here comes Smoky." A light gray and white gull landed on the railing. "Where've you been?" She brushed the bird's back and smiled. "Meet my new friend."

John nodded and whispered, "Hi, Smoky."

"Watch this." She adjusted her blouse to expose her pocket. "Show my friend what I taught you."

The seagull hopped down onto the arm of the wheelchair and plucked a cracker from Nancy's pocket and flew out of the gazebo.

"It took me over a month to get him to do that." She grinned with pride and closed the screen. "That's enough for now. They'll be coming in after our food."

The constriction in his throat fought against the words he was trying to say. "You're a gifted young lady."

"Thank you." She went to the table. "I almost forgot." She opened a cabinet and brought out a large handmade greeting card. "I made this for you."

"You drew this?" He studied the front of the card.

"Those two seagulls are Ricky and Lucy. They're smooching like I saw you an' mom doing." She giggled.

"You saw us?"

"I peeked out the front window and got Aunt Clara in trouble."

John opened the card and read: *I'm glad you make my mom happy.* The card was signed: *Nancy* in big, bold blue letters. The greeting was centered inside a large red heart. "This is a treasure." His voice broke and tears came.

"You're crying. Do you feel sorry for me?"

"No. Not for a single second." He wiped his eyes on his sleeve. "I'm overwhelmed by you an' upset with your mother."

"Why?"

"For not telling me about you. For not letting me meet you before this."

"She was afraid you'd see me an' run away."

"Well, I'll tell you what, little angel, that's never going to happen."

"You mean it?"

"With all my heart." He moved closer. "May I hug you?"

Nancy started to cry. "Yes."

He held the child. "I'm so blessed to have met you."

"Me too."

John sat back. "We're going to have so much fun."

"With Timmy too?"

"Yes, with Timmy too."

* * * *

Carolyn drove in and spotted John's VW. "This is not what I had planned." She looked in the rear view mirror. Sandy pulled in behind her.

Chapter Fifty Three
Resolution

THE GAZEBO – AT THE SAME MOMENT:

Nancy moved her wheelchair up to the table. “I promised Aunt Clara I’d set out the plates an’ stuff.”

“Let me help.”

“Okay, that’ll be fun.” She smiled. “I knew you’d be a nice man.”

“Thank you. I like to think I am.” He took two plates from the stack and put them on the table where Nancy couldn’t reach.

“There are napkins and cups in the cabinet by the grill.” She sped her chair around beside John. “Hand me the cups.”

"Okay." He handed her two mugs. "You're pretty good with that chair."

"I get in trouble with it sometimes. That's why mom had this place and the ramp built." She took two more cups on her lap and spun around to the other side of the table. "I wanted to be closer to the seagulls and this thing doesn't work too well in sand." She laughed.

John put a large package of napkins on the table. "How many people are going to be here?" He watched her arrange the place settings. "Your mother didn't tell me."

"There's you and Timmy, Aunt Clara, Mom, Aunt Sandy and little old me." She smiled and her eyes sparkled with pure joy.

"You know what?"

"What?"

"I've known you just under an hour ... and I think you're the most precious, prettiest little girl I've ever met."

"Thank you. Now I know why Mom likes you."

* * * *

Carolyn and Sandy stepped into the backyard and watched Timmy and Clara walking down the ramp. The boy carried the picnic cooler and Aunt Clara followed with the Crockpot.

Timmy shouted, “Here comes food.”

Carolyn tensed and whispered, “I didn’t want it this way.”

“Leave it alone.” Sandy grabbed her arm. “It happened. You can’t change it.” She held Carolyn back.

John came out of the gazebo and took the heavy cooler from Timmy. “I got it.” He went back inside and put it down next to the grill.

Carolyn stood stone still. A slight wind ruffled her hair. “They didn’t see us.”

“That’s a good thing. Take some air and relax. You’re as stiff as a board.”

“I wanted to introduce them.” She drew in a long breath.

“You didn’t and they’ve met. By the looks of it, things are just ducky. Don’t spoil it.”

Nancy’s laughter drifted out of the gazebo and swept a smile across Carolyn’s face. “Okay. I’m all right.” She hugged Sandy.

Clara plugged in the Crockpot and looked up. “They’re here.”

John opened the cover on the grill, turned to see the two women walking down the ramp. Sandy came in first. “Hi, I’m John.”

“I know. Pleased to meet you.”

He rushed by her and went to Carolyn. “I can’t believe you.” He threw his arms around her. “Why?” He squeezed. “Why didn’t you tell me?" His eyes filled. "Why?"

"I couldn't."

"You damn well should have." He pressed her against his chest and kissed her on top of the head.

"I was afraid you wouldn't understand."

He pulled her away and held her by the shoulders. "Understand what?" He used the back of his hand to wipe his eyes. "You didn't think I could deal with a child?"

"Nancy's different."

"You bet she's different." He gestured toward the gazebo and whispered, "That little girl of yours is the most wonderful, gifted person I've ever met." He raised her chin and kissed her.

"Are you sure, John?"

"I'll give you a hint." He smiled and wiped his eyes again. "Nancy, Timmy, you and me are gonna do so many things and have so much fun together you'll have trouble catching your breath."

She hugged him and let go of her pressing tears. "I want to believe you."

"Well, you can. Any child who talks to a seagull and teaches it to take a cracker from her pocket is a phenomenon. I want you and Nancy in my life."

She can be a real handful and she's not

always so sweet and nice."

"Neither are you and neither am I."

"Do you have a napkin?"

"Fresh out."

She wiped her eyes on his sweatshirt, looked up at him and kissed him. She studied his face and smiled. "I love you, John Freeman. I love you with all my heart."

He looked down at her and swallowed a short breath. His words came out in whispered pieces. "You have no idea how I've ached to hear you say that. I fell in love with you the first time I saw you. I thought you were the most beautiful, nastiest bitch I'd ever met, but I loved you anyway."

She kissed him on the chin. "Let's join the crowd and have our barbecue."

"Okay if I play chef?"

"Be my guest."

"One thing."

"Yes?"

"When we wrap this cookout, may I see you alone?"

"Absolutely."

Chapter Fifty Four
The Gift of Love

TWO HOURS LATER:

Timmy poured a Coke over ice and handed the cup to Nancy. "I was close to a no-hitter last Sunday."

"You're kidding."

"No. Really. We were at the top of the sixth and I had this kid down by two. I wound up and let it fly. Wham—he smacked it straight through center field."

"Wow! I wish I could've been there."

Timmy looked at John and Carolyn. "We're playing tomorrow. Can you guys bring Nancy?"

"Mom, please."

Carolyn grinned and nudged John. “We’d have to take your other chair.”

“No. I’ll use the crutches. I can. You know I’ve been using them.”

John took a breath. “You don’t need the chair?”

Carolyn squeezed his arm. “Your chair would have to go along anyway.”

“Okay, but I can use the crutches. I promise, I’ll be careful.” She beamed and poked Timmy’s arm.

John looked at Carolyn. “Is it all right?”

She smiled. “I think so.”

He sat back and took a sip of wine. “It’s a done deal.” He grinned. “Nancy, if I have to carry you all day it will be my pleasure.”

“You would do that?”

“I give you my word.”

“Yea!” Nancy and Timmy slapped a high-five. “I’m gonna see you pitch.”

The boy took a drink of soda. “You guys are the best.”

Sandy and Clara came down from the house. Clara started clearing the table. “I have a big batch of peach cobbler in the kitchen whenever you’re ready.”

Sandy pulled off the tablecloth and folded it. “I’ve had two helpings and it’s great.”

Carolyn took the half-full wine bottle off the cabinet next to the grill. “Nancy, why don’t you and Timmy go up to the house. Have some cobbler and watch TV. Okay?”

“You two want to be alone, right?” She smiled wide.

Sandy leaned toward John and held out her hand. “It has been a pleasure to spend this afternoon in your company.”

He stood and shook her hand. “I’m flattered.”

“You have no idea how important this day has been for all of us. Thank you for being the man I’d hoped you’d be.”

“I’ll try to live up to all of that.”

“I’m sure you will.” She looked at Carolyn. “I’m happy for both of you.” She gave John a hug and kissed him on the cheek. “Thank you.” She nodded. “You two need some time alone.” She followed Nancy and Timmy toward the ramp.

“Hey, Tim.”

The lad turned back. “What?”

“The Padres are playing a doubleheader on Monday. How about Carolyn and I take you and Nancy to the games?”

“For sure?”

Nancy turned around “Really?”

“Remember, Timmy, I have the tickets.”

Nancy squealed. "Mom, can we?"
"Yes, child, yes we can."

John added, "Get permission from your mom, Tim."

"It's in the bag." He gave Nancy another high-five.

A FEW MINUTES LATER:

John and Carolyn walked out onto the beach from the stairs behind the gazebo. The setting sun had started sliding into the ocean at the distant edge of the earth. The constant wind had fallen still and allowed the end of the day a moment of golden peace.

Carolyn pushed the wine bottle into the soft sand. "Let's sit here."

"Works for me." He handed her the glasses. "Half in mine."

The surf whispered its never ending concert and played a haunting refrain to a large group of sandpipers that danced along the edge of the incoming tide.

Carolyn poured a half glass of wine for John and another for herself. "Do you have any idea of the joy you gave Nancy today?" She took a sip. "Not to mention the feelings you opened in me."

"That child has a treasure of happiness in her little heart. I didn't do anything to add to what she already has." He twisted his glass into the sand. "I'm glad I got to you." He brushed hair from her face. "I prayed for it."

She put her glass in the sand. "You prayed to get to me?"

"Yes. I had fallen in love with you." He sat up and stared at her. "I wanted you because I could feel something from you. I didn't know about Nancy. You weren't telling."

"I told you, I couldn't."

"It doesn't matter." He took another drink. "We're here, we've had this great day and you were afraid of it."

"Eleven years, John—I've sheltered Nancy." She turned away and looked into the fire in the sky. "I put my little girl in that wheelchair."

He watched Carolyn's tears fall and appear as tiny flames on her cheeks.

John brushed her hair. "How did you do that?"

"I got into drugs and rampant sex. I camped out in communes. I got pregnant. Nancy was born in some emergency room I can't even remember."

"How did that put her in the wheelchair?"

"She was born with spina bifida." Carolyn covered her face with her hands. "Nancy may not live past eighteen."

He sat up straight. "There are treatments. I know that." He pressed her left hand to his face. "We'll get her the best." He moved closer and put his arm around her. "I know some people at the university."

"Nancy's getting the best care possible. There is no cure."

A cool breeze rushed in from the surf and twirled sand around the stems of their wine glasses. It sent a chill across the back of John's neck. "There's ongoing research. They could hit a breakthrough anytime."

"You sound like Nancy's specialist. He keeps telling me the same thing." She pulled a napkin from her jacket pocket and wiped her eyes.

"Is there any improvement?" He kissed her on the cheek.

"She's stable and we're living with that right now." She looked at him and read the sincerity in his eyes. "Are you sure you want to get involved with all of this?"

"What? You and your beautiful daughter?" He poured more wine in each glass. "It will be a blessing to be part of your lives. I met Nancy just a few hours ago and she immediately filled my heart with her innocence and love."

Carolyn brushed her hand through his hair and smiled. "Why, John Freeman? Why are you this wonderful gift that came running out of the morning fog and into my life?" She smiled and finished her wine.

"I think Timmy has to take some credit for that. He introduced us."

She sat up and stared out at the remains of the setting sun. "You volunteer time to work with mentally challenged children instead of being involved with healthy kids that play sports."

"What's wrong with that?"

"Nothing. Let me finish."

"I'm listening." He sipped a little wine.

"There's a motive behind that and I'd like to know what it is."

He stood and looked down at her. "The bottle."

"I think I just hit a nerve." She handed him the wine.

John poured what was left into his glass and dropped the bottle on the sand. "What I'm about to tell you is never mentioned in my family or outside of it." He hunkered down in front of her. "My younger brother was born with Down Syndrome. Paul died while I was in Vietnam. I cared for that angel while we grew up. Ballgames, drive-in movies, Saturday picnics." He drank some wine and laughed. "I even took him on a weekend camping trip. That was a total riot, but Paul got a kick out of it."

Carolyn blotted her eyes. "I knew there had to be something."

He moved and sat beside her. "I was crawling on my belly at the base of some goddamed hill I never heard of when my little brother died. My squad was running reconnaissance in the middle of the night. We were ordered to pull back."

"Okay, John. That's enough."

"You asked, I'm telling you." He downed the last of his wine. "When we reached base camp, I got the word. Paul was dead."

"I'm so sorry."

"I flew home and on the plane I read the last letter my little brother had sent me. My mom had helped him get the words right. I'll never forget it. Hi Sonny, I know you do good there. Come home soon, I miss you. I'll keep that letter for the rest of my life."

"I understand."

"Here's the motive you wondered about." He leaned forward and hugged his knees. "I went back to Huntsville, Texas to kneel before a hunk of stone that has my brother's name engraved on it." He watched the day fall into the sea and turn off the light.

Carolyn gripped his upper arm. "You don't have to say any more."

"Yes, I do. I promised myself I would reach out and be there for as many handicapped children as I possibly could. That's why I work with Angels Unaware."

"You have filled my heart, John Freeman. I can't believe it."

"Believe it, Lady. Be prepared to have me and Timmy filling Nancy's life with as much happiness and joy as possible."

"What about me?"

"We'll put you on the list of events."

"Oh, you will?" She pushed him down and kissed him. "I'm gonna love you to death, Mr. Freeman."

"I think I can handle that."

Epilogue

FOUR MONTHS LATER:

Steve came back from the portable bar with two drinks. He handed one to John. "You have about an hour. Getting nervous?"

"I've been shaky for the last two days." He took a sip of gin and tonic. "I want to thank you again for agreeing to give her away."

"I'm pleased she asked me." He sat at the small table alongside John. "The changes in Carolyn since you two got together are amazing."

"She's made a major difference for me too."

"Who wanted to have the wedding at home?"

"Carolyn. She needed it small and I agreed, but I thought she should have all the trappings anyway. She deserves it. The gazebo is where I met Nancy for the first time. We decided that's where the service would be."

"Good choice." He held up his glass. "To you for making Carolyn happy."

* * * *

Aunt Clara looked out through the kitchen window. "The caterers have the tables set up. They'll be bringing food in here any minute."

John's mother started clearing the center island. "I'm still dizzy from that long plane ride. I hope I don't drop anything."

"You want to sit down for a minute?"

"I'll be all right if I just keep busy."

* * * *

Timmy waited in the living room with Nancy. He handed the rings to her. "Okay, I'll be standing beside John. You give the rings to me and turn off to the left."

"Yeah, I got it."

"Don't speed down the ramp like you did yesterday."

"I won't." She giggled.

"Don't do that either or you'll start me laughing."

Sandy walked into the room. "Timmy, it's time. You go down to the gazebo and stand next to John."

Nancy smiled. "Aunt Sandy, you look beautiful."

"Thank you. Wait till you see your mother." She adjusted the white silk pillow on the child's lap. "When you hear the song start, go down the ramp slowly."

"I know. Don't speed an' give the rings to Timmy."

"Perfect. I'll be walking right behind you. Okay, we're ready."

* * * *

Roberta Flack's song The *First Time Ever I Saw Your Face* filled the gazebo. John squeezed Timmy's hand.

The minister smiled. "Are you ready, John?"

"More than I've ever been for anything in my life." When Nancy got closer he whispered, "I love you."

Carolyn stepped in behind Sandy. John filled with emotion.

Her stunning white, ankle length gown glowed in the afternoon light and her smile radiated from deep in her heart. She whispered, "I love you, John Freeman." She held a long stemmed rose from which all the thorns had been trimmed.

About the author

Ted Tillotson lives with his family and Eight rescued feline friends in Central California.

Readers may contact the author at:

http://www.tedtillotsondragonlairbooks.com

www.ingramcontent.com/pod-product-compliance
Lightning Source LLC
Chambersburg PA
CBHW070357260626
47161CB00001B/171

* 9 7 8 0 6 1 5 4 7 0 4 7 4 *